UP S

By

Max Chennault

Son of the fabled Claire Lee Chennault,
father of the Flying Tigers

With Flying Tiger tales from the legendary David Lee "Tex" Hill, Ed "Kid" Rector, C. Joe Rosbert and from many 14th Air Force greats including John Alison and Wiltz "Flash" Segura.

CASTLE BOOKS

Memphis

The American Heroes Series

UP SUN!

The American Heroes Series

Compiled by Wallace Little with Charles Goodman

ISBN 0-916693-14-7

CASTLE BOOKS
P. O. Box 17262, Memphis, Tenn., 38187

". . the tapestry of memories . . ."

Thank thee, God, for the tapestry of memories that we all share, with dark threads of death in the cockpit and death in a cradle. Memories with glimmery gold threads of joys we had together, so many experiences with those in an ancient land. We thank thee, dear Lord, for freedom, that priceless gift. As we pause tonight to remember those who gave their last full measure of devotion, we also honor those men with us yet who made history by their courage and valor and sacrifices that this freedom might remain intact.

-- *A prayer by Mrs. Betty Blackstone, a missionary friend of the Flying Tigers, at a 75th Fighter Squadron reunion in St. Louis.*

Pieces of a legend . . .

The ecstacy and the agony of trying to make love in the back seat of Jeep sitting on a cold China hillside; a young man searching for his missing fighter pilot father; desperate kitchen surgery behind enemy lines; loving care given by a missionary's wife, slipping through enemy lines in *coolie* disguise after being shot down in flames, shooting a comrade in the head as the flames of his burning plane creep toward him, pinned in the wreckage.

Here are true air war stories, told by the men who lived them. Some stories, like their tellers, are really funny. Some are heart wrenching and tense. All entertain with breathtaking reality.

Many who read my book, "Tiger Sharks!" published by Castle Books of Memphis, wrote they would like to see more stories from the men who lived them in the China-Burma-India Theater of World War II.

I sent out the word and stories came back from generals, group commanders, pilots, doctors, air-crewmen, and men in ground support. One delightful piece came from Max Chennault, the son of our fabled leader, General Claire Lee Chennault who formed and trained the famous Flying Tigers who later were the foundation of his 14th Air Force.

China was so different from any other war theater that it is difficult to put in writing.

Our leader was involved in a bitter personal dispute with no less a man than the theater commander himself, Lieutenant General Joseph Stilwell.

"Vineger Joe," as the theater commander was called, knew a lot about directing troops in trenches - some said he was "the best 4-star squad leader the U. S. Army every had - but he knew next to nothing about the uses of a modern air arm. He seemed to care even less.

As a result, Stilwell permitted only a bare bones supply of planes, fuel and maintenance equipment to get to the Flying Tigers and the 14th Air Force, even though they were the only American force then winning victories. America's other forces were being mauled and put to shame everywhere else in the world.

We fought Japan's forces in China to a standstill on a shoe-string - or less.

The fighter planes sent to us were mostly obsolete or worn out machines, discards from other theaters of war, tired aircraft that were more suitable as a hard stand display in a museum than active combat.

Often there were not enough repair parts to get battle-damaged planes back in the air. When they did get patched up, they often were grounded by a lack of gasoline.

It was a strange war and the stories which follow, somehow, manage to capture what it was really like.

Even when the stories are funny or weird or tragic we recognize them to be true. Little details testify to their authenticity. Anyone who has not served in China could not possibly have written them, or even supplied the basic facts about these events. As one writer said, "You had to be there."

May these tales bring you happy reading - a smile, a tear and a frequent laugh, as they did to me.

UP SUN!

The American Heroes Series

CASTLE BOOKS
Memphis

Flying Tigers Up Sun

By Max Chennault
College Park, Georgia

Editor's Note: Did Claire Lee Chennault fly his plane into combat against the Japanese before America officially declared war on Japan? His son, Max, says he did. Max says his father took on the Japanese air force - alone at first, later having to be content to send his young Flying Tigers "up sun" - that favorable fighting position high in the sun above enemy planes where Japanese flyers would be blinded when they looked up in search of their attackers.

There can be no question. Dad flew combat against the Japs.

I'm told that Nationalist Chinese war records show that Dad shot down 55 Jap planes. The Chinese government paid him $500 bounty for each plane he shot down. That's the money he used to put me through college.

The Chinese government opened up an account for Dad at the Chase Manhattan Bank in New York City in early September of 1937. Dad had been over in China only three months.

His contract said the Chinese government was to pay him $1,000 a month in gold. Within three months, Dad had $15,000 in the account. Where on earth did the rest of that $15,000 come from? I'm convinced Dad earned it by shooting down Jap planes at $500 a shot.

I've read those stories that tell how he stood off to the side, merely watching the combat, but I don't believe them. If there was anything he ever wanted to do, it was take a shot at them. He thought he was the greatest pilot in the world and he might have been close to the best fighter pilot. He wrote a manual on it.

There were eight of us kids in the original family before he married Anne and had two more.

I never saw my dad drunk. He rarely cursed and he hated anybody who lied to him.

We used to play bridge all the time. He taught us when we were about 10 or 11 years old and we lived out in the Hawaiian Islands.

"You kids almost through with your home work?" he'd say. "Let's have a couple of rubbers of bridge."

We were pretty good. He didn't mind taking any one of us on.

We played auction bridge. Contract bridge had not been heard of then.

"We're going to put up some prize money tonight," he would say. "The first place winner gets 15 cents. Second place gets a dime. Third place a nickle. The one with the least gets the experience."

He was "real generous," putting up 30 cents. He knew he wasn't going to lose much. The whole thing would cost him maybe a nickle. He figured he was going to win the 15 cents top money and mother was going to win the dime and so it was going to cost him a nickle to play cards.

If one of the kids did win the 15 cents or the dime, he'd say, "Well, you outfoxed the old man tonight."

We loved to play bridge with him.

He was a real smart man. His mother died when he was 5 years old and he used to go to his Aunt Lou's house. She had a lot of patience and a couple of kids of her own. She spent a lot of time with Dad, taught him to read, write, to do arithmatic. He started going to school the year his mother died and he graduated from high school when he was only 12.

Dad said he went through the first, second and third grade in the first year. He started to Louisiana State University when he was only 14.

None of us were ever as smart as he was.

He and mother got married when he was 17 years old. She was older - from January 21, 1893 to September 6, 1893 older - than Dad was. He told people he was older than he was because he didn't want them to say, "Good God, he has all these kids and he's little more than a boy himself."

Dad called me "Mike." The other kids accused me of being his favorite. I was 17 months younger than brother Jack. Jack played the piano and read a lot, and he played tennis. He didn't like to get out and hunt deer and ducks and things. He later flew a P-40 in the Aleutian Islands and was a fighter wing commander. He said he shot down a Zero with floats on it.

We went out to Hawaii when I was 9 years old and came back in September of 1926, a month before I was 12.

We moved back to Louisiana. One cold, December morning - it was down near freezing - Dad said we were going to hunt ducks and squirrels.

I went with him to one of the bayous. Dad had a strange way of knowing exactly where he was at all times. Me, when I got 50 yards away from where we parked the car, I was all turned around and lost.

We were walking down in the woods and we heard a strange, "Ooooh, oooooh, oooh."

We were down on the Tensas River.

I said, "Dad, what in the world is that?"

He started running toward the sound. "It's wolves swimming across the river down there. Come on."

I yelled, "Let's climb up a tree."

He yelled back, "I'm going down there and see if can head them off and shoot 'em."

Sometimes we would stay out hunting until it got slap dark. Dad had studied squirrels and discovered something about their habits. They always fed right before dark. Knowing that about them, Dad said the squirrels would just mess around until then. You might get a stray shot but most of them would be moving around pretty good.

Dad liked to study the habits of the things he hunted - like the Japanese fighter pilots, later on.

Dad bought a Savage rifle and took it down to a gunsmith and had an ivory bead put on the front end of the barrel. He could see that ivory bead late into the evening.

He shot squirrels in the head.

Once, down at Kelly Field, he had gone up to give a final check ride to a pilot and when he came home early that afternoon, he said, "Come on, Mike. I think I know where some ducks are. Let's go get 'em. I was flying around and I looked down and saw this little pond and I saw two ducks. Let's go get 'em."

When we got to the area, he parked the car and said, "Stay here."

He had noticed the wind direction and figured out the whole thing. He figured which way they would take off, going up wind. He crawled on his belly over the little hill and there were six ducks. He had five shells and one in the chamber.

He got every one of them. He was fabulous.

He came from some good hunters. His father used to go out quail hunting with a pistol. Dad said his father could shoot five times and get two birds on the rise.

He left us at home and began commuting between the United States and China.

He also left with us his dog Joe. In China he had trained Joe to go retrieve whatever he shot.

One day at home, I looked out and saw two ducks sitting on the lake and I got my shotgun and killed them for supper.

Joe Dog swam out in that cold water and brought one back to me. But I couldn't get that little rascal to swim back out in the cold lake and bring in the second duck.

Dad happened to come down to see us a couple of days later and I said, "Dad, that darned dog of yours isn't worth a damn."

I told him Joe would not go out and get the second duck.

"Well, he always gets them for me," said Dad. "Maybe it was the water being so cold."

I said, "I had it figured that he wasn't used to anyone killing two ducks at the same time."

Oh, he glared at me. What a dirty look I got!

Later on, I was working as an air traffic controller down at West Palm Beach.

There was a Captain Blythe down there and he called me in the tower one day and said, "I got a C-47 going to China. You want to send your dad a bottle of booze?"

I didn't have a bottle with me in the tower at 6 in the morning, of course, but the captain said he could pick up one at the officers club at Morrison Field. He called me back in a few minutes and said he had a bottle of Johnny Walker for me and he'd send a Jeep over to pick me up so I could take the bottle out and give it to the C-47 pilot, a guy named Whitey and he had a Chinese copilot with him named Moon Chin.

About a month later, I got a letter from Dad. It was early spring of 1944 in China. He wrote, "Whitey delivered the goods. I'll use it one of these days to celebrate a great victory. I'm sorry you didn't know I was a bourbon drinker and I really don't care much for Scotch. Next time, if you want to send me something, send me some okra, shrimp and oysters and I'll have my Chinese cook make me some Louisiana gumbo."

In February, here came another letter from him and he said, "I really enjoyed your Louisiana gumbo but I had a heck of a time teaching my Chinese cook how to make it."

Dad liked to take me up as a kid and do loops and rolls and stalls and banks until I got real sick and threw up all over the back seat.

Fifty years later, it was June 19, 1954, I went for another ride with him in his old Douglas 38 at Maxwell Field. I told him I could still feel how sick I was at times.

"Do you still remember that?" he said.

He did it to me the first time in 1938 at at Brooks Field in San Antonio. We were flying an old Consolidated PT11.

I was riding behind him and I reached over and hit him. He looked back and smiled and said, "Made you sick again, didn't I?"

When we got back on the ground, he said, "You bring a dollar with you?"

I said, "What's the dollar for?"

He said, "You must pay a mechanic to clean up the airplane."

The Shinchiku Raid

By David Lee "Tex" Hill, San Antonio, Texas

Editor's Note: General Robert Lee Scott called the Shinchiku raid "the greatest mission we flew in China."

Since returning to China in November of 1943, after General Chennault called me back from Eglin for a second tour, I had been thinking of Shinchiku.

Shinchiku was Japan's big military airdrome that sat facing China on the coast of Formosa, a big island just 94 miles out into the East China Sea.

It was truly was a tantalizing target. It had never been within the range of our P-40s. Now that we had some of the new P-51s, Shinchiku had come within our range - but just barely.

I talked to Bruce Holloway about it in India. I ran into him down there when he was leaving to go home and I was flying back in. Bruce had commanded the 23rd Fighter Group when Bob Scott left, and now Bruce was going home and I was assuming command of the 23rd and working with

Colonel Casey Vincent who commanded the 68th Composite Wing. Bruce had told me there was a big raid in the works. He told me a little about the deal but he said it was a very secret thing and I would be in on it.

Bruce told me he had flown a photo recon plane over Shinchiku and come back with pictures of more than 100 fighter planes and bombers parked on the ground like a big flock of sitting ducks.

"Destroy them on the ground," the Old Man always told us, "and you won't have to face them in the air."

We knew that we would have to have the advantage of total surprise. If the Jap defenders at Shinchiku had only a couple of minutes warning, their fighter squadrons might be able to launch an armada that would destroy us. We couldn't even talk about it to our own pilots.

However, if we could break the Shinchiku defense, it would change the whole tone of the war. The island was the key to the inner defense system of Japan. It was the empire's main transshipping center between the home island and the southwest. It was a combat training center. They also made bomber modifications there.

"When do we go in?" I said.

"The weather recon planes are watching the coast over there," Casey said. "Thanksgiving Day looks pretty good to 'em at the moment. That could change any minute. Weather is unstable on Formosa at this time of the year.

"We need a good day when we can make it all the way - in *and* out."

If we could sneak across the stretch of water between the coast and Shinchiku without being spotted, we could do an awful lot of damage. Of course, if they spotted us on the way in, it would be like walking right into a hornet's nest. Our navigation had to be perfect. Everything had to work. It had to be a perfect mission - or it could be total disaster.

The day came. The weather was good and it was holding. Visibility was perfect.

In darkness on the eve of Thanksgiving Day, we slipped in, one by one, to our advance airfield at Suichwan, 250 miles east of Kweilin. It was a key field in a chain of advance bases we had just finished.

Fourteen B-25s from the 11th Bomb Squadron flew in, late in the evening. The light bombers would do the navigating for us all.

The pilots were all asking questions but we gave them no explanation. No hint.

I brought in eight of the P-51s out of the 76th Fighter Squadron. I brought in eight P-38s from the 449 Fighter Squadron that had come out of Africa.

Thanksgiving morning, at daybreak, they got us out of bed. Everybody got up, anticipating something but they didn't know what was going to happen. We briefed them around 9:30, showed them pictures of the target, and 30 minutes later we were gone - on our way.

It was 420 miles to the target.

One B-25 didn't make it because of engine trouble.

When we crossed the China coast, we dropped down to just above the waves so radar couldn't pick us up. That also made us less visible to shipping that might spot us and flash a warning.

The P-28s would lead he B-25s in and my P-51s would follow to mop up anything still in the air or sitting on the ground and not already smoking.

It was 94 miles over water, all of it on the deck, and we didn't even have a life jacket. I never saw a Mae West in China until the bombers got there and I saw their crews wearing them. Later, I sweated, just thinking about crossing that much water on the deck, strafing and coming back on the deck - with no life jacket.

I placed Sam Palmer and his P-38s on one flank of the light bombers and I led the P-51s on the other flank.

Teddy White, the war correspondent, was up in the nose of Lieutenant Colonel Joseph "Preacher" Wells' lead B-25. White was planning to write a story about it for *Time* magazine.

The flight over the water took only a few minutes but it was long enough for the palms of my hand to start sweating on the stick.

Then it rose like a pale strip of shadow out of the ocean - we had hit Shinchiku right on the nose. Just before noon. Right on time. We climbed to about 500 feet.

I was thinking, "Noon on Thanksgiving Day. Everybody is sitting on the ground down there eating turkey while we sit up here like turkeys."

As we approached. I saw a transport plane coming down the shore line and I dispatched a P-38 and he went up and shot the transport down just as we hit the edge of the beach where the big airdrome sat waiting.

There was an unbelievable number of bombers strung out into the distance, single file. They were in a landing pattern that stretched back for miles. They had their wheels down and were just coming back in from a mission. Below them, the airdrome had all the gasoline trucks sitting out on the field. Their ground personnel were out there waiting to refuel the planes - just an ideal situation for us.

Sam Palmer and his P-38s climbed to about 1,500 feet and went in strafing and then started in on the bombers.

I switched to my main fuel tanks and dropped my auxiliary gas tanks under my wings just before hitting the coast. I climbed to about 500 feet and brought my Mustangs in behind the bombers to protect them from an attack from the rear when they came streaking over the field - 14 bombers flying abreast at about 1,000 feet - dropping fragmentation bombs on long rows of hangars with the bombers parked around them.

We came across the field in a clean-up strafing run. We set fire to more of the parked bombers and nailed a couple of fighters struggling to get up into the air. Those guys looked up at us out of their cockpits with the most surprised look on their faces.

We were just knocking them out of the line like birds going down with their feathers on fire.

Seven Jap fighter planes were just coming off the ground and I got one of them. It was an Oscar. He came off the runway and pulled up on a steep left climbing turn. All I had to do was raise my nose a little and fire. He just exploded. The guys behind me got all the rest of them.

Then the P-38s came back down the line at the airdrome, strafing and raking the parked bombers and then they pulled up as a top cover for our B-25s.

The devastation was really something.

The bombers flew through the smoke and flames of all the planes that the P-38s had set on fire. What a scene for Teddy White in the nose of Preacher Wells' plane.

B-25 gunners were chewing chunks out of everything they passed and ripping the ground crews who were in a panic, running about in search of protection. The B-25s banked away, giving their gunners a shot at the barracks and they took out another couple of Zeros still in the air.

As we turned and climbed out I looked back. I counted about 20 bombers burning on the ground, and smashed and smoking heaps of fighters, a couple of transports and one German Stuka dive bomber scattered around the airfield. Hundreds of ground personnel lay bloodied all over the place.

We regrouped over the water and headed back across the straits. Man, what a relief. Just then a round cooked off in one of my guns because the barrel was so hot. I thought some Jap had got in behind me and I *jinked* the plane in a reflex action and my left wing dipped and damned near went in the water before I could pull it out.

We still had a lot of open water to cross but I began to feel good.

Casey Vincent was waiting by his radio back at Kweilin for word of how things had gone. If we had run into big trouble I was to call the code words, "New York." If it went well, I was to say, "San Antonio," which was my home town.

We only had a bullet hole in one of the P-38s and there was some minor damage to four of the B-25s.

I opened my radio transmission. "San Antonio - in a big way."

A big yell went up in the limestone cave back at Kweilin when they heard it.

Our recon fighters had taken pictures on their last pass over the airdrome and when we got back, our photo intelligence people came up with one frame that showed 37 Jap planes burning.

All our planes made it back even though we were at the extreme range of fuel.

It was one of those dream missions.

In Japan that night, they knew their inner ring of defenses had been broken.

The Rest of the John Dunning Story

Editor's Note: Remember the B-25 that went over the end of the runway at Chihkiang, crashed on the river bank below and burned? Don Lopez and I both wrote about it in our books - but there was more to it than either of us knew. What everybody already knew was that John Dunning had mercifully shot a young airman in the head who was facing a cruel death, trapped in a burning B-25 after we all tried to pull him out but couldn't get him loose. It created a lot controversy when it was reported back home in Time magazine.

It came up again at the September 3, 1989 reunion of the 75th Fighter Squadron at the Crystal City Marriott in the District of Columbia. At the reunion, one of the men in the hospitality room caused everyone there to get suddenly quiet when he started coming up with new information on the incident:

"John and another pilot had gone through school together. They grew up together. They went off to college together. They flew with each other through flight school, and got their wings and their commissions together. For the next few years, they had different assignments, but when they hit China, they were both assigned to the 5th Group, China Air Corps Wing. Dunning was the CO. By that time, he was a light colonel. His friend from childhood days was a major. They flew a lot of missions together in China. Sometimes they'd go out separately, each leading a mission.

"One day while Dunning was up, the 5th got a frag order to hit another target. Remember, CACW still had 'forties, and we were still having trouble with water in the gas. Well, the major got the 'in commission' list from the maintenance people, and assigned planes to each pilot. They went out to their planes, and cranked up. They made their engine run-ups okay, then started their takeoff runs down the Chihkiang strip to the south, as usual.

"The major led. He was barely airborne when his engine quit. He slammed the plane back on the ground and tried to get it stopped before going off the south end into the river bed, the same spot the B-25 went off later on and burned.

"When the major saw he wasn't going to get his plane stopped, he shoved the nose into the gravel runway and cartwheeled. But the plane came down on its back. The major was pinned in the cockpit. Fuel spilled out and the hot engine ignited it.

"Chihkiang had no fire-fighting equipment. We had no equipment to lift the plane to get to the cockpit to free the major. In a couple of minutes, the plane was a roaring inferno.

"In a short time, we saw that the major was no longer moving. We only hoped he hadn't suffered too much.

"Later, when Dunning landed and we told him what happened, he was greatly upset. He called a meeting of all personnel in the unit, and told them that no matter what, if such a situation happened again, they were under his orders to shoot the man rather than let him suffer and burn to death."

"That explains why John didn't hesitate later on to shoot the kid trapped in the B-25," I said.

"That's right," he replied. "He wished someone had done that for his friend."

Tail End Charlie

By J. Roy Brown, Rockport, Texas

A Jeep is the worst place in the world to make love in.

I know, I know. There is no bad place, just some places better than others. I've listened to liars and braggarts describe how they got it in every conceivable position or place from aboard the back of a camel to rail fences. No doubt they did. But I still maintain that for sheer misery and frustration and physical discomfort, nothing beats a Jeep for exquisite torture of graveled knees, sprains from contorted limbs, and bruises produced by trying to have sex in the back seat of a Jeep in a cold drizzle at 6500 feet elevation.

But youth and the stoneache form a powerful incentive for mischief. When combined with a 22-year-old in the Back Of Beyond who hasn't seen a white woman for over a year, it can be explosive to the point of idiocy.

In 1943 I was a fighter pilot temporarily based at a ratty place called Yunnanyi, located on the Burma Road in the high Himalayan foothills of far western China. We operated missions into Burma and Siam, that presumably gave protection to the Burma Road convoys and the steady stream of air transports hauling supplies from Assam, India to Kunming, China. My P-40 was named "'Ole Hellion" and my Jeep, shared with others, was called "Charlie." Charlie was the vehicle leading to my learned conclusion about the unsuitability of Jeeps as make-do love-nests. I got into plenty of scrapes with Ole Hellion, but my most memorable event was my lusty effort with a jolly Red Cross girl in the back end of Charlie.

After landing from a trip to Burma one chilly, drizzly day I was debriefed in the Ops Hut along with other pilots when I suddenly hallucinated. I had experienced this before, as had others. It consisted mainly of spots before the eyes among which strolled a nude beckoning woman. This was what I saw now in the middle of the Ops Hut. Only this time it was no hallucination but real - but they were wearing clothes.

Two desirable, delectable white women walked in, not nude and not beckoning, but women and *white*. They were dressed in a sort of flight suit that is now called a jump suit. They were cute as hell. American girls.

I was speechless!

"Hi, fellows," they said, and I gaped. So did everyone else.

I turned to my boss and CO, Bob Polk, and feebly pointed at the visions. Bob chuckled and said, "This is Clara Benson and Bonnie Richards. They are assigned here by the Red Cross as this base is being expanded."

Everyone gathered round them but suddenly we were shy and embarrassed. Shy because the appearance of white women was so sudden and unexpected, and embarrassed by the naked thought in our prurient minds that just had to be tangible and visible to the girls. But they were poised and at ease, personable and humorous.

I was never a sex-hound. Of course, I had the normal urge and yen for it but lacked nerve and assurance around women. I didn't like to dance, and was an unsophisticated sort of lout so most of the time, back in school or service in the States, I yearned from the sidelines, and envied the jocks who could snap garters with impunity and casually take their pick of the flock. I listened to their bragging tales of steamy conquest with jealous envy but with disgust also. Not from their alleged acts, which I admired, but the bragging about it, which seemed a bit below the belt. It always seemed to me that sleeping with a girl should be a private thing and not made a topic for public discussion.

On those rare occasion when some sympathetic or desperate girl helped initiate me into the juicy mysteries of sex, I most thoroughly enjoyed and appreciated it, but kept silent afterwards. That probably had as much to do with the illusion of keeping her for myself as it did with ethics, but I felt better for it anyway.

All that changed. My new sex life became public property with the advent of Clara and Bonnie. I found a new boldness inspired by excessive horniness. I drew a dead-set bead on Clara, plump, laughing Clara. She was amused and matter-of-fact at first and parried my clumsy perspiring moves casually as she had countless others.

"Yipe!" she said, "I never saw such a bunch in my life. Philadelphia was never like this. Is everybody this horny? Bonnie and I have been on bases before but this beats all!"

"Who's bothering you?" I panted. "I'll kill them all!"

She laughed and slapped my hands away.

"Just stop it now. No one bothers me or Bonnie either, except you cocky fighter pilots. Everyone else is so nice and respectful it hurts. But everywhere we go, tongues are hanging out a foot and every eye is undressing us. It's nice to be wanted but this gets embarrassing. I feel sorry for them, so many, so long away from home, some of the men for years, poor things."

I swore, and growled, "Never mind those others. Feel sorry for me."

Time, persistence, threats of violence to other equally eager guys, and one near rape, finally prevailed. Clara, worn down by the relentless chase, became at least partially agreeable but she was dubious about the logistics of the thing.

"This is no good," she protested. "Where can we go? There is no privacy anywhere. You sleep in a rat-infested room with other guys and Bonnie and I share a room, such as it is. There's no hotel in this crummy place, stop that, and its cold and rainy, stop that, so we can't do it outside now, stop that!"

But all that jazz was unimportant to me compared with the main objective.

"Forget all that stuff!" I groaned. "Lets go to your place. Bonnie is playing Red Dog with Polk and the others. It won't take long. Please. PLEASE, Clara!"

Reluctantly, she consented but was ill at ease at the thought of Bonnie returning unexpectedly and refused to undress completely. "What if . . ." she began, but I gave that malarky no thought at all and peeled both of us like a flash and got right down to it in a hurry.

She said, "Just a minute, Buster. You take precautions. No, wait, now, LISTEN . . . !"

So, furiously I grabbed a condom from my pants on the floor and fumbled with it. I couldn't get the blamed thing unrolled. I was having a fit.

"Here," she giggled. "Don't have a seizure. Let me do it." And she expertly rolled it on and off we flew - into the wild blue nowhere.

Her experience was greater than mine in several ways, including interruptions in a shared room. Just as she feared, at the crucial moment voices sounded outside. The door opened and Bonnie and Polk walked in. Both had flashlights on. Clara's wail coincided with my wild leap for my pants.

Later, I had a session with Polk. I cussed him good. "You could have gone somewhere else and let me finish. I'll never be the same . . ." My string of adjectives made it sound like I hated him. Actually, I didn't. We were good friend, but he sure upset me this time, and I was letting him know it.

Polk just grinned and protested, "Hell, we didn't know you were there. All you had to do was tell us and we would have stayed away. Anyway, you'd better get set up for a trip to Lashio tomorrow. Take wing bombs."

Man, I was suffering! That cruddy, cursed . . .

The Nips at Lashio must have thought their gods deserted them, the berserk way I attacked them with bombs, then strafed them repeatedly and furiously.

"Hey, Klondike," my element leader finally called. "Hey, Loverboy. How 'bout us knocking it off before we run out of fuel and ammo, hey? We can't kill all the cruds and anyway, these bums didn't interrupt your piece of tail."

The whole squadron knew about it. That so-and-so Polk! I'd kill him. But first I'd nail Clara. Some way. Somewhere. Somehow.

Bet on it.

But not right away. Next day, I was sent to South China with a flight to raid Hainan Island, Haiphong, Hongay and any shipping we could find. Mess up everything we could for the Nips. So my pursuit of Clara had to wait a few weeks. Upon my return, I was determined to set things right and make up for lost time.

Clara was waiting when I landed back at Yunnanyi, and greeted me as if nothing had happened, which it hadn't.

Not yet.

"What's the good word, Clara?" I got right down to it. Had to. Pressure was high and rising fast.

"Have a good trip, Tiger?" she asked. "Get caught with your pants down again? I heard you did." She laughed.

She was referring to a fouled up mission to Hainan that got my airplane all shot up and scared the juices right out of me. "Forget that," I thought.

"Where can we go?" I inquired. "Quick. And let's do it right this time. I'm a basket case from that other mess." I was in a sort of hurry.

"That's all up to you, Laddie. You can figure that out but it had better be different from the last time, I can assure you, because we aren't going to fool around again in my room."

"I've got it," I said, inspired. "My Jeep. We'll take Charlie and go up the road. Then those sorry jerks can't crash in just as I'm . ."

But she interrupted. "What? It's cold and rainy, and I'm not getting out in that wet, muddy grass, so forget it."

I could tell Clara wasn't nearly in the bind that I was. Wet grass didn't seem all that bad to me.

"No, no," I reassured her. "We'll stay in the Jeep. People do it everywhere. It's no different from a car and half the people in the world were conceived in the back seats of cars."

But she was still fretful. "It's a lot different. That old Jeep is so tiny it doesn't even have a back seat, just some metal things. And its full of mud and almost no top and . . ."

But I was fed up. I was very eager, and in no mood to listen to further drivel. We got into the Jeep and drove off.

I told Polk we were going into town for dinner so he would know where we were. He raised an eyebrow and chuckled. "Tony Harriman and I will let you use our room if you like. We owe it to you." Harriman commanded another squadron in the group, and was a real sex-hound when he had the opportunity. I was so eager I nearly grabbed at it, but then I reconsidered. Clara wouldn't be comfortable knowing two other sex-mad clowns were probably standing outside listening. While that wouldn't have deterred me, I didn't trust them not to walk in or have half the squadron singing "O'Riley's Daughter" or "The Good Ship Venus" or some other bawdy song to serenade us.

With all the dignity I could muster, I said, "Go screw yourself, Polk. I'll do this my way."

He laughed.

Then I left.

There was only one road, the Burma Road, running through the squalid village. There was a so-called restaurant there frequented by U. S. personnel who were brought to town in a Chinese charcoal-burning truck.

We took Jeep Charlie and headed down the road. Clara leaned over and kissed me and patted my knee. "You poor guy. You're all wound up. Relax and enjoy it." She kissed me again and I sizzled.

"Uncork that jug of plum wine in the back and lets have a drink. Then let's stop," I suggested.

"You drink if you want to, but I wouldn't touch that awful stuff."

I took a healthy belt, holding my breath. That wine burned with a bright blue flame, killed bedbugs on contact, and would gag a mule. I took another jolt of it, then pulled off into a relatively level spot and stopped.

"Not here, you fool. Someone might come along. Besides its misty and cold. Let's find a better place."

"Nah. Not tonight." I took another slug of that jing bao juice, and barked like a fox."

"Not here! Not in this lousy weather."

"Don't worry. Everyone is working or on an early mission tomorrow. Come on, Clara, let's get in the back." I jumped out.

"Oh, alright, you jackass. I've never known anyone so single-mindedly obsessed as you are. But I'm not going to undress here."

That no longer mattered. I was ready to bore right through a girdle or even armor plate by now. We got in the back and I started fumbling around trying to get into position. Clara was right. It *was* cramped. She squirmed and twisted, trying to get comfortable while I charged right ahead.

She giggled.

"Look at your feet. You must be a contortionist."

It dawned on me that I was practically paralyzed. I looked back and my feet were turned up at an impossible angle against the back of the front seat, which was pushed forward, while my knees were grinding into the gravel and mud on the floor. I was bent in sort of a backward bow. Clara was half in, and half out of the Jeep, and her poor feet and legs were wet and cold.

It was a glorious . . . mess!

"We can't stop now, Clara," I panted as I moved my feet, causing the back of the front seat to slam me in the butt. I had to stop and turn around and push the seat out of the way, then start all over.

"My back's killing me!" Clara gasped. "All my circulation has stopped and something is cutting into my hip."

"Stay with it, girl!" I wheezed. "Pop goes the weasel anytime now."

Headlights came on, and a horn squawked as a truckload of soldiers stopped along side of Charlie.

"Need any help, Cap'n?"

"Wow! Look at that butt! Give her one for me, Cap'n."

"We'd better get out of here before he starts shooting at us!"

"Good luck, Cap'n," and they left, trailing ribald cat-calls as they went.

Clara groaned. "Of all the damned stupid things I let you talk me into, and I'm cut and scraped and skinned all over. Let's go home."

I picked the gravel out of my knees and tried to get a kink out of my back and said, grimly, "No way! I've heard getting it in Jeeps is a common thing now, and we aren't gonna let anything stop us now."

What a blast!

But I had to admit that I'd never been so exasperated trying to get a simple piece of tail. Clara laughed until she got hiccuping. The next day I had swollen knees and a sprained back, and walked like an old man.

Polk and Harriman laughed, and said, "You dope, why didn't you take the rice straw mattress off your cot and put it in the Jeep? You got a lot to learn about back-country sex."

I thought I'd already learned a lot. I felt great. Jeep Charlie was unaffected.

Well, I had to go back to India to bring back the first P-51 into our area. From that and moving to another base, I only saw Clara briefly after that. She asked me to bring back for her some fancy pink things she called shoes, but I called them slippers. She had seen them in Calcutta. I got them and brought them back. I gave them to her, and a jug of Hayward's gin as well, when she met me at my plane.

She kissed me and said, "Look, I hope you will come back, and thanks for the shoes. And listen, that Jeep wasn't so bad, and we'll do better with practice. You come back."

I never saw her again. Whoever married her later was a lucky guy. I doubted if she ever introduced him into the intricacies of having sex in the back seat of a Jeep, however. If she did, once his knees stopped swelling and returned to normal, he probably remembered it with a grin.

I still hold that a Jeep makes a lousy lovemaking couch.

But I'd try again.

Editor's Note: This story is a chapter from Brown's book in progress.

My Cajun Roots

By Wiltz "Flash" Segura
New Iberia, Louisiana

Editor's note: General Segura delighted his fellow Flying Tiger Association members with banter like this at a Squadron 75 reunion dinner in St. Louis:

I'm a Cajun, you know. A Cajun is a descendant of French Canadians in the province of Arcadia. They are smart - but they go to a lot of trouble hiding it.

When Irish immigrants first came to America, they were not too much thought of. They had jokes like, 'Who lit the fuse in Mrs. Murphy's Tampax?' Then they got an Irishman in the White House so now they begin telling Texas Aggie jokes and Texas A & M became the most popular school in the United States.

Then Pollock jokes started and now we got a Pollock in the Vatican.

Now, the Cajuns saw this and so they started telling Cajun jokes and the first thing you know, they made a Canjun general - and I'm it.

One day they told my Cajun friend, Boudreaux, "Boudreaux, you can't get a job because you just got a bad body odor. Watch on television. They'll tell you what to do."

On television they told him all about a man's deodorant and said, "Put it under your arm."

Two weeks later, they ask Boudreaux, "Did you get your job?"

"Yea, but I lost it," Boudreaux said. "Every time I raise my arm, that deodorant bottle fall down."

One day my dad bought a $35,000 bull and turned him loose in the pasture with the cows. That bull lay down in the shade. My dad called the vet and told him and the vet said, "Don't worry. I'll send you some pills. Give him one a day."

Dad gave him a pill and the bull made love to all the cows in the pasture. The next day he gave him another pill and that bull jumped the fence and made love to all the neighboring cows.

The farmers all saw this that they came running over and said, "Wonder why he's doing this?'

Dad said, "It's something in these pills."

"Well, what is it?" they asked him.

Dad said, "I don't know but it tastes like chocolate."

And then a Canjun blind man came in the grocery store with his seeing eye dog. He grabbed the dog's tail and twirled him around.

The grocer said, "What are you doing?"

"Oh, I'm just looking around," said the Cajun.

A Cajun lady went in the hardware store next door to look for a hinge.

"What kind you want?" asked Boudreaux, the clerk. "Big? Small? What?"

"I'll take one of them medium hinges," she said.

"You mean, one to put on a cabinet door?" Boudreaux asked.

"Yes. One of them hinges to put on a cabinet door."

So, Boudreaux gave her one and said, "Now, you wann'a screw for that hinge?"

"No," she said, "but I will for that microwave over there."

My Cajun friend, Tibido, was at the beach in Hawaii watching the girls. A girl in a skimpy little swim suit came up to him and she said, "You like a smoke?"

"Yea," said Tibido. "You got one?"

She unzipped a little and reached inside her little swim suit and got one and Tibido lit it up.

She said, "You like a drink?"

"You got that, too?" Tibido asked.

She unzipped a little lower and reached in and got a little bottle of Vodka.

They talked a while and she said, "Would you like to play around?"

Tibido said, "You got some golf clubs in there, too?"

Down at Cape Canaveral there were a bunch of Cajun boys working and they all got fired. So they went to see their minority representative at NASSA and he told the authorities, "You can't fire all the Cajuns like that. They have their rights, too."

"But we had to," the NASSA people told him

"Why is that?"

"Well, every time we say, 'Prepare for launch,' they all sit down and start opening up their lunch sacks."

One day the Cajuns left the proving grounds and went back in a swamp and cut down a big cypress tree and hollowed it out and stood it up on end and began working on it.

The people at NASSA heard the Cajuns were building a space rocket so they went back in the swamp to check on it.

When they saw the big round cypress trunk standing on end, they shook their heads and asked, "Are you boys planning to go somehwere in that thing?"

"We go to the sun," said Tibido.

The NASSA men shook their head and said, "You boys are crazy. Don't you know the sun is hot? That thing is wood. It would burn up when it got close enough."

Tibido said, "No, no. You NASSA boys all think you are so smart. You think Cajun boys are crazy. We are not going to burn up. We wait and go up there at *night*."

It's easy sometimes to misunderstand. A Cajun boy walked into a lumber yard and said he wanted to buy a 4 by 2.

"How long do you want it?" asked the clerk.

"We want it for a long time because we're going to build a house."

Another Cajun went to visit a friend in a hospital. All the hospital beds were full. People were lying in the halls, on stretchers, everywhere. The Cajun boy wanted to do what he could and he asked a patient, "Can I help you in any way?'

"Ling ha, hong foo, boo ha," said the patient.

"Look, can I help you? Just tell me that." said the Cajun.

The patient gasped once and fell dead.

When he got back home, the Cajun boy went to a Chinese restaurant. He asked what that had meant: Ling ha, hong foo, boo ha.

The Chinese waiter said, "That mean, 'MOVE! You stand on my life support system!"

Missionary Tales

By Mrs. Betty Blackstone
Pasadena, California

Bill, my husband, and I were with the Presbyterian mission in Hunan. We had gone out to Peking in 1931 to learn Chinese. My husband was brought up in Nanking. His parents were Methodist missionaries so he had the language already and spoke it fluently.

Our mission in Hengyang was behind a stone wall about ten feet high. The chapel and the hospital opened on the street. Our mission houses were inside the wall, behind the hospital. We also had a school where I taught boys English, music and the Bible. I trained our little choir. I was the educational missionary and Bill was the evangelistic missionary.

The boys from the Flying Tigers came by for dinner almost every night. Hospitality was part of our mission. If the boys got sick they could come over to our hospital.

Flash Segura had black hair and he'd come over at night - at any hour. He was good medicine. Always full of jokes. He saw the funny side of life. He kept everybody's morale up.

John Alison, who later was Madame Chiang Kai Shek's personal pilot, would come when the Madame came to Hengyang. She would come over and stay with the Frank Newmans at the hospital. Frank ran the hospital.

We had three children. Not long after our youngest, Virginia Lee, was born, a great big, tall sergeant came to see her. He was an airplane mechanic and had just got the news from back home that he was the father of a new baby boy.

He said his boy was 21 inches long. He wanted to see Virginia Lee and that would give him an idea of what his little boy looked like.

He came straight from the flight line and he was still grimy and his hands were dirty. But he had to see Virginia Lee.

I just didn't have the heart to say, "Look, we wash with soap before we touch an infant."

Jennie Lee got pneumonia when she was about three months old. She was alrealdy wheezing when the sergeant picked her up.

She died in less than a month.

The boys felt they had to do something. So they began picking camelias that grew wild everywhere. It was the only flower blooming then. As they sat around the alert shack, waiting for their planes to come back from missions, they would weave these camellias into nice designs for Jennie Lee's funeral.

They made several lovely wreaths and a big camellia cross and brought it over one night. They were the flowers Jennie Lee had at her funeral.

The boys got cleaned up and put on their uniforms and dressed for the funeral. They acted as Jennie Lee's pall bearers. Big guys, carrying that little baby in a casket that was only a straw basket.

We buried Jennie Lee inside the compound and put a little marker on her grave.

After the Japs drove us out, one of the boys asked his pilot to fly over the compound, low enough to see if the grave marker was still there. He told us a Japanese barracks had been built over Jennie Lee's grave.

We left Hengyang and went down to Sung Jo because we were being bombed so much. The communists had burned our old mission there when they broke with Chiang in 1924 so we had to build a new house.

The boys gave our son, Bob, an aircraft spotter's guide so he could identify planes going over. He was good at that.

One night a plane began circling overhead. We figured it was Japanese because American planes always flew straight on.

The children were asleep so we grabbed them up and ran for the bomb shelter.

Bob woke up and he heard the plane circling over us. He said, "Where are we going?"

"To the bomb shelter," Bill told him.

Bob listened and then he said, "That's a new sound. It's not a Japanese plane. It's a B-25."

Bill said, "Are you sure?"

"Yes."

The Chinese headquarters was just across the street from us.

"I'll run over there and tell them it's an American plane," Bob said.

Bobby went with him. Everybody got a lantern and ran across town to an emergency airfield and lined the runway with their lanterns.

Our boys in the circling B-25 had been on a bombing run at Hong Kong. They dropped half of their load on the first run and when they came back in on their second run they had been blown off course by winds that were near typhoon force.

All they knew now was that they were over land and not over water but they didn't know if it was controlled by Japanese troops or if it was friendly.

In the dark, they saw the train station that was all lit up, waiting for the train that was coming through at midnight. The B-25 dropped down and the pilot was going to try to land on the railroad tracks. He was running out of gas.

As they were coming down, one of the crew saw the dim little rows of lantern lights lining the little runway where Bob and Bill and the others waited across town. So they swung over there and landed safely.

When they stepped out of their planes they expected to be captured by Japanese troops.

But there were Bill and Bobby greeting them.

It was a strange world in many ways.

My husband and Ted Romi, another chaplain, decided one afternoon to go down and see which of the Flying Tiger boys would like to come to our home for dinner the next evening.

The children, Bob and Margie, wanted to go with them. I was reticent about their going. There was going to be a full moon that night. That meant the Japanese would bomb the Flying Tiger base.

"We'll be back early, long before dark," Bill promised me.

While they were still visiting at the Flying Tiger base, the Japanese came in on a bombing run and the bombs began dropping all around them. The flyers ran for the slit trenches while Bill and Ted grabbed up the kids and ran to the edge of the river. There were two sampans there.

They operator of the first sampan refused to take them on board. He had a superstition about the River God. He said that, if you deprive the River God of his prey, you are responsible for the person you saved for the rest of their life. The sampan operator said he didn't want that kind of responsibility for Ted and Bill and the two kids.

They found the other sampan operator and he said he would take them so they all jumped on his sampan and away they shoved out into the dark river.

Bobby was lying under a mat, near the rear of the boat, and, after they got far out in the river, he kept saying, "I hear water coming in the boat."

Finally, Bill took his flashlight and looked down through a crack in the floor. Sure enough, water was coming in. It was up near the top of the boat.

The sampan was sinking. The river was a mile wide. It had a powerful current.

As the sampan started under, Bill grabbed up Bobby. Ted picked up Margie. Bill asked the sampan crewmen if they could swim. Two could. One said he couldn't.

They all jumped out and began treading water so they wouldn't be sucked under when the sampan went down. And they started yelling for help.

The Japanese bombers were coming over and they were dropping bombs on the base. Above the bombs, Myron Levy, the Flying Tigers adjutant, back at the base, heard men and children calling for help from out on the dark river. He ran down to the edge of the river and found another sampan sitting there. The owner refused to go out on the river at night.

Myron pulled out his .45 and said, "You go."

Just as Bill and Ted could hardly keep their heads above the surface any longer, holding the kids in their arms, Myron and the sampan operator pulled them out of the water. They found two of the sailors but the third one who couldn't swim was lost. They dragged the river for him the next day but never found him.

When Bill and the rest of them finally got back to shore, several of the boys were waiting for them with blankets and they wrapped them up and took them to the slit trenches until the bombing stopped. They finally got back to our compound late that night.

I Saved Joe Dog

By John Alison, Washington, D. C.

Editor's note: At Kweilin, one of the small bungalows, little more than sleeping quarters, was set aside for General Chennault when he visited that base. Kweilin was in the Central China valley, and much of the offensive operations of the 14th Air Force fighters either originated from this base, or was directed from it. John Alison was commander of the 75th Fighter Squadron, which at that time, was based there. General Chennault came to visit, one time, and today General Alison remembers this incident:

Nights were dark at Kweilin, not only because of the limited power of the gasoline-powered electrical generating units. They were kept dark in order to prevent the Japs from locating the base by its lighting pattern and making surprise attacks.

The darkness sometimes led to amusing incidents.

On one occasion, General Chennault and Joe Dog, his pet dachshund that always traveled with him, came to Kweilin.

My cabin was right next to his so he could get me pretty quickly if he had something on his mind.

That night, as usual, after dark, all visible lights were turned out.

Leaving the lighted mess hall that night, I walked out into a pitch black night. I had to grope my way along the paths that led to the cabins that were located about 50 yuards from the mess hall.

I could hear Joe Dog barking up a storm. Nearing my own quarters, heard the General, standing on the veranda of his bungalow, calling to his dog.

"Here, Joe. Come on, boy. Where are you? Come on, boy. Here Joe. Come here, Joe."

Joe kept barking. The General kept calling to him in the dark.

From near me in the darkness, came a snort which I recognized to have come from Joe Dog.

I at once realized what the situation was with the dog.

"He can't come to you, General," I called out in the darkness.

There was a moment of silence.

Recognizing my voice, the General asked asked softly, "Why can't Joe Dog come, Johnny?"

"I believe Joe he has fallen in a hole, sir," I said.

Another moment of silence in the darkness. The General had not known I was out there listening.

"What makes you think Joe would fall in a hole?" the General asked.

I hesitated, then told him.

"Because I fell in it myself, last night," I said.

The night before, I had come groping back along the path through the dark, on my way back from the mess hall. I had put one foot out in front of me and felt nothing at all under me.

Fortunately, the men digging a cesspool pit had left a board down in the bottom of the pit and I stood it up against one side of the pit and was able to climb out.

I told the General I thought I could get Joe out of the hole.

I found the edge in the darkness and eased over the side and dropped into the hole. I scooped up Joe Dog and felt around some more. The same board was still standing against the dirt wall, right where I had placed it the night before.

I was glad the General never told anyone about that incident.

Last Day at Liuchow

By Ed Rector, Arlington, Virginia

Editor's Note: This story is from Colonel Rector's own book in progress titled, Memories of a Flying Tiger.

On my return to China for my second tour, in October of 1944, I was assigned to the 68th Composite Wing. The 23rd Fighter Group, plus other units of the 68th, had borne the brunt of the valiant but futile effort to stem the slow but measured advance of the Japs southwest along the Siang River Valley. Hengyang, Lingling and Kweilin, all key bases, had fallen to the Japs.

That was the situation when I arrived at Liuchow in early November of 1944. I was assigned as assistant wing operations officer and was immediately involved in ongoing evacuation activity.

On the eve of our final departure, our intelligence reported the enemy 20 miles away and advancing.

It is best to insert here a problem the 23rd faced. It was now a four-squadron group, with the addition of the 118th Tac Recon Squadron. The 118th was equipped with P-51Bs and used by the 23rd as a regular fighter squadron. The rest of the group was equipped largely with P-40Ns and therein lay the challenge. The N, the last in the line of a great fighter plane, had a couple of shortcomings: a fixed wooden seat with no vertical movement, and an electric needle and ball presentation as a basic instrument flying capability. One could do a two-needle-width turn, return to level flight and the turn indicator stayed at two needle widths deflection!

The weather at Liuchow had deteriorated in the remaining three days and P-40Ns were flying west to Luliang, and elsewhere, on the wing of C-46 transports, the latter climbing at a minimum speed of 135 mph so that the Ns could maintain formation. The 118th transports and several Ns remained, to depart for Luliang on the final day.

The ceiling was now a solid 400-500 feet but with relatively good visibility, four to five miles.

Lt. Col. Edward O. McComas, commanding officer of the 118th, had devised the final fly-out plan most effectively and he carefully briefed all pilots involved. The three-plane flights, led by a P-51B, would take off to the north, followed by two P-40Ns. The flight would assemble in a tight formation on a long down wind, then head up the takeoff runway. The flight would then start a climb to 8,000 feet, due north, then turn west, climbing to 12,000 feet, the cruise altitude to Luliang.

I briefed my two wing men in further detail:

• Take off on internal fuel.

• On downwind, and before join up, check proper feeding of your belly tanks.

• You have one hour and fifteen minutes, plus or minus five minutes, of external fuel.

• We will be in cloud virtually all the way to Luliang.

• At one hour after takeoff, I will give each of you a thumb and forefinger twisting motion. Switch to internal fuel immediately.

We proceeded per plan and promptly at one hour I gave the switch signal to my left wing man. He reached down momentarily, then gave me a thumbs up. I gave the same signal of to my right wing man just as we encountered moderate turbulence. I got back full time on the gauges until we smoothed out, then checked him again.

I waggled my thumb, in essence asking if he had switched to internal fuel. He gave me a thumbs up, chewing gum and grinning happily.

What soon occurred is beyond belief - but it happened.

At 1:12 elapsed time, we suddenly broke out into a great amphitheater of clear air, with clouds above, below and all around us. I turned left to give a smile of assurance to my left wing man and right to do the same thing. To my horror, his propeller started slowing!

I throttled back as quickly as possible, bearing in mind that I had another wing man, and nosing down simultaneously. We stayed abeam, losing some 300 to 400 feet altitude. His prop caught again and he pulled back into formation about four seconds before we reentered cloud on the far side.

We broke out into clear weather 30 minutes later and landed at Luliang without further incident. My right wing man, a red-headed second lieutenant, was still chewing gum but the grin had disappeared!

Some musings:

This was a serious and demanding undertaking, yet the young redhead grinned confidently through most of it. I know he learned from failing to switch to internal fuel. I trust and hope he is alive today, enjoying life serenely but with an added appreciation of attention to detail.

Although we encountered occasional moderate turbulence, other flights met severe turbulence and thunderstorms. The 23rd lost four P-40Ns on this endeavor: three bailouts and one went in.

Final thought:

Is there such a thing as Fate? Why did the red head exhaust his external fuel just as we entered an amphitheater of clear air? Why did he catch up, bare seconds before we entered cloud again? Five seconds difference, either way, and he would have been in deep trouble.

I don't know the answers.

Goat In Pinks

By W. O. Fisher, Palos Heights, Illinois

We had been in China a long time. Maybe *too* long. All our clothes had been lost in transit somewhere between Florida and the Far East. We were wearing shirts and pants made of some kind of stuff that looked and felt like poorly refined burlap. We had these made while we were in India. It was all we had. My shoes had been made by a street cobbler in Karachi. We still had our Air Corps A-2 leather flight jackets and flying suits but that was all that remained of our GI outfits, issued and purchased.

The four of us - Carl Hardy, W. F. X. Band, George Meachem and I - were a little tired of it all by late 1943.

To make matters worse, we started getting replacement personnel who outranked us. Among them was a First Lieutenant Howard Whitehurst, a man who became a very special case for us. Not only had he been promoted ahead of us while still serving in the Training Command before he came out to China, but he arrived with a well-stocked wardrobe of the best officer uniforms.

Whitehurst kept his clothing in the best Stateside shape - his pants and shirts had creases sharp enough to cut butter. Every evening Whitehurst would show up for dinner, dressed in his crisply pressed uniform, his tie neatly knotted and his cap, just as if he were dining at the Randolph Field Officers Club. We showed up in our home made clothes or in our flying suits, all sweaty and greasy from long use.

The contrast between us and Whitehurst was really startling and irritating.

One day we knew he was on the flight schedule and we knew he would be away from his room on a mission for at least five hours. We decided to take advantage of his absence.

There was a big goat that hung around our unit at Chengkung. Band, Hardy, Meachem and I were at the alert shack and knew fairly exactly what time Whitehurst's flight would return, and how long the debriefing would take. About an hour before we expected him to land, debrief and return to his room, we went out and captured a big goat and led him back to Whitehurst's room.

We tied it to the stove in the middle of the room. Then we took Whitehurst's pinks and proceeded to dress the goat in them.

We put the legs of Whitehurst's clean, creased pants over the goat's back legs, pulled the pants up over his body, tucked in the shirt and buckled the belt around his waist. We buttoned the top button of the shirt around the goat's neck, put on Whitehurst's necktie, and affixed his hat to the goat's head. Even if I do say so myself, the big goat looked pretty neat and sharp.

We heard Whitehurst's flight returning to base. Shortly after, we finished dressing the goat and tied it again to the stove with a short leash. Then we all retired to our own rooms. Just before leaving Whitehurst's room, I snapped a picture of the goat.

A few minutes before Whitehurst arrived back at his room, the goat messed in his pinks.

Whitehurst strode into his room, looking forward to a refreshing shower, donning his crisp, clean pinks and heading for dinner. And, when he entered the room, there was the goat, resplendent in his pinks - with the seat of the pants soiled and really sagging.

To describe Whitehurst as irate would be an understatement. Whitehurst was so angry that, had he been able to identify the culprit, there might have been some blood shed. For some unknown reason, he accused everyone in the squadron but those of us who had actually done it to him.

Soon after, Whitehurst was in a fight over Kunming in which his flight leader, Lieutenant Clapp, led them up into about 80 Zeros. In the fight, a shell hit Whitehurst's plane, passing over his shoulder and exploding in the cockpit. It caused some severe cuts on his face, and blew off parts of several fingers. With blood running into his eyes, and spurting from his hands, he somehow managed to land that plane. The doctor told him he was physically unqualified to continue in fighters. They assigned him to the Air Transport Command. He continued to fly in China.

The next time I saw him was years later at a reunion in Atlanta. Knowing he was to attend, I brought along the picture I had taken of the goat, fully clothed, waiting in his room. After swapping stories for some time, I gingerly recalled the event and asked him if he would like to see the picture. By this point in time, Whitehurst had learned to live with it and he thought the photograph was real funny. I offered to send him a copy after I got home. He said he had never found out - until that moment - who had dressed that goat in pinks and had never suspected I was one of the culprits.

John Hampshire

By Wallace Little, Fort Walton, Florida

John Alison, a retired Air Force major general, thinks John Hampshire might well have been recognized as the greatest United States ace of World War II had he lived.

Alison was the commander of the 75th Fighter Squadron when Hampshire was assigned to it and remembers Hampshire reporting in to him in the fall of 1942. No slouch as a fighter pilot himself, Alison personally tested every new pilot coming into his squadron to find out his capabilities.

"Single combat with the Japanese was highly unprofitable and forbidden by General Chennault because of the superior maneuverability of the Zero," recalls Alison. "But simulated fighting with another P-40 gave me a good idea of the another pilot's skill. When I first flew with Hampshire, his capability in formation was exceptional. It was relatively easy for me to best most of the pilots in individual combat because of my senior experience, this was not so with young Captain Hampshire. On our first try, it was all I could do to keep from being roundly defeated. I held my own, but recognized that here was a pilot of unusual skill."

Alison said he noticed from the beginning that Hampshire had a highly competitive spirit, a strong desire to win and was an exceptional aerial gunner.

Ed Goss, a later commander of the 75th, told of Hampshire's exploits on one mission:

"Our fighters had become separated while trying to contact with the enemy, and I was overtaking the Japanese formation from the rear as their bomber started its run. I was closing in, had the bomber in my gunsight. Before I could pull the trigger, the bomber exploded.

"While I had been coming up from the rear, Hampshire approached the enemy formation from directly ahead and picked their lone bomber right out of the center of their formation."

In early May of 1943, Major Goss got a special assignment from General Chennault, and Colonel Alison came back in to take over the 75th Squadron temporarily.

"When you fly and fight with men for almost a year," said Alison, "you develop strong attachments and I was looking forward to a return visit."

It was during Alison's brief stay with his old squadron that Hampshire was killed.

Ed Goldman of Portland, Maine gives us this background on John Hampshire who came from Grants Pass, Oregon:

Out of high school, Hampshire worked at a gas station to help put himself through Oregon State College, take flying lessons at the Grants Pass Airport and earn a commercial license to fly. He enlisted in the United States Army Air Corps and ended up as a flight instructor at Kelly Field in San Antonio. He was assigned to pursuit pilot duty in Panama and then in Puerto Rico, and was elevated to the rank of captain. He arrived in China in September 1942 and was assigned to then Lieutenant Colonel John R. Alison's 75th Fighter Squadron.

Alison credited his young captain with 17 confirmed kills before he was KIA on 2 May, 1943 at Changsha, while he was still only 23 years old. John was buried in the American Cemetery in Kunming. He was later reburied at our National Cemetery in Hawaii.

The Day "Hamp" Died

By John Alison, Washington, D. C.

Early in May 1943, I had a chance to spend a few days with my old squadron, the 75th. Major Ed Goss had a special assignment from General Claire Chennault, and I was to replace him on a temporary basis, which gave me an opportunity to spend a few days with the troops of the 75th. When you fly and fight with men for almost a year, you develop strong attachments, and I was looking forward to the visit.

I had been with the squadron only a day or so when our telephone air-raid warning net reported 47 Zeros approaching. During the previous few days we had been sitting around stretching the truth a little and telling each other how good we were. I'm sure we weren't nearly as good as we thought we were, but it is terribly important for a fighter pilot to feel that way about his business.

John Hampshire had a great sense of humor and was always kidding.

The Japanese used a peculiar squirrel-cage kind of formation when they made a fighter attack on our airdromes. On this occasion, Hampshire told me how he intended to join the formation and not come out until he either broke it up or was shot down. He invited me to join him, and bet me I would chicken-out before he did. He was kidding me about this as we walked out to our planes and took off. The warning net reported the 47 airplanes coming down from the north and about 100 miles away.

On this day the 75th had 16 airplanes in commission, manned by seasoned pilots. Sixteen P-40s with expert pilots against only 47 Zeros seemed to us to be kind of unfair to the Japanese. In the earlier days of the war we had often been outnumbered as high as ten-to-one. On this day, we were all in good spirits and anticipating giving the Japs a resounding beating.

I positioned the 16 airplanes above and to the side of our airdrome at 18,000 feet.

I don't know what happened to the Japanese formation, but only 10 or 15 Zeros came forward on reconnaissance. They crossed the airdrome about 8,000 feet below us. I thought it must be a trap. I waited a few minutes until the reports from the warning net indicated that the rest of the formation was not going to commit itself, then we attacked. Either my aim was poor or the Japanese pilot I engaged was skillful because I failed to score after expending considerable ammunition.

Everyone scattered in the melee.

Then five of our pilots assembled on my wing, and I started north to take on the main body of the formation, which according to the reports was retreating toward Hankow. Inflight reports told of about five or six Zeros claimed in the action.

Hampshire came up on my wing, reported one kill, and said I'd find the wreckage one mile off the north end of our runway. And there it was when we went out later to investigate. This was Hampshire's 16th victory. Although his life was to end a few short minutes later, I was able to confirm his 17th victory before a lucky or skillful shot by a Japanese pilot put an end to his career.

As I led my small formation north there was lots of chatter and excitement and chatter on the radio.

Hampshire was betting I'd never overtake the Japanese. About 100 miles north of our airfield we encountered a thunderstorm and let down to about 500 feet to pass underneath it. I saw three Zeros hugging the earth ahead and making for home. As we bored in, Hampshire went underneath and pulled up in front of me while I was firing, and we both missed the flight leader. But his two wing men, who were tucked in tight, hit the ground simultaneously. It was a spectacular start.

I'd been so intent on the three sitting ducks that I missed seeing a larger formation of Japanese above us. They attacked and there was adequate confusion until it was over a few short minutes later - six Zeros were down and we formed up again to return to base.

When we counted noses, Hampshire was missing. We'd been fighting over the edge of a broad river which emptied into a lake near the city of Changsha. One of our pilots said he'd seen a plane dive vertically into the lake; another contradicted this and claimed an airplane that looked like a P-40 had landed in the water near the river bank. There was some confusion as the pilot who saw the aircraft go straight into the water insisted it was a Zero, while the one who saw the aircraft land in the water insisted it was a P-40.

Some of the confusion was cleared up shortly after we landed at our own base. I received a message from the Chinese command post in the Changsha area. It was brief and shocking. Brutally translated into English, it said simply: "AMERICAN PILOT LANDED IN RIVER. HIT IN STOMACH, GUTS RUNNING OUT. SEND DOCTOR QUICK."

I don't have the talent or understanding to explain the feelings of John Hampshire's friends. One of his most devoted friends was our flight surgeon, Ray Spritzler, who announced that he was going to John's assistance. Someone suggested that we stuff the doctor in the baggage compartment of one of our fighters and let him jump out near where John went down.

At this time, and under the stress of emotion, I didn't realize how hazardous such a venture might be. I consented and we made the doctor as comfortable as possible in the cramped quarters of the fighter's baggage compartment, which was not designed to accommodate a human being. The door was removed and a signal arranged between the pilot, Lieutenant Joe Griffin, and Ray to indicate the time to jump. A signal such as wobbling the wings or shaking the aircraft had to be used to enable the pilot and doctor to communicate.

We saw them off. It was not until they departed into the northern sky where storms had begun to gather that I realized this wasn't such a good idea. I grew truly fearful when a few minutes after their departure we received a second message from the Chinese saying that Hampshire had died. We tried to reach Griffin on the radio, but electrical disturbances caused by thunder squalls to the north made this impossible.

I spent an anxious hour or so waiting for them to return, and finally just as it got dark we got a report from our warning net that a lone airplane was approaching. At the time, we didn't know it but Griffin had run into severe weather and had been unable to reach Changsha. Griffin was now trying to get back home before dark, for after nightfall, landmarks on the Chinese countryside vanish and we had no radio navigation. Also in his part of China there was no utility system, and therefore, no electrical lights. Our runway was outlined by a thin row of flare pots fueled with tung oil. Their feeble lights would give the pilot an outline of the runway for landing, but they couldn't be seen for more than a mile. We heard in the distance what we took to be Griffin's airplane droning through the dark. We tried to reach him on the radio and give him directions, but the intensity of the static made this impossible.

Hours passed and no reports. I computed the time when they would have run out of fuel. Then my heart really sank. I composed a radio message to Chennault reporting that I had lost Hampshire, but I didn't have the courage to tell him that I had lost another airplane too, and possibly another good pilot and my doctor because of my own poor judgement. I decided to wait out the night, in the hopes that before morning we would have a report as to where the plane had crashed and that some miracle had preserved two good friends who were risking their lives for another good friend whom they couldn't save. That night I prayed for forgiveness for my stupidity, and prayed for help which I knew in my heart couldn't come.

Morning came and still no word.

Several hours after we had positioned and manned our aircraft down on the flight line, I decided that I had no alternative but to let General Chennault know how stupid I had been. I was composing my report when someone shouted, "Here they come!" and a fighter plane touched down on the airfield, taxied up to the flight line, swung around, and there was Ray Spritzler's smiling face peering out of the baggage compartment.

Their story was unbelievable. Completely lost and almost out of fuel, Griffin decided to abandon the plane. But just before giving the signal to jump he spotted a cluster of lights on the ground. Any lights probably meant a village, and Joe reasoned that there might be a telephone down there and that, if he circled, this would be reported to the Chinese warning net and at least we would have a fix on the area where they had abandoned their aircraft.

As he circled the lights, he noticed to his amazement a long stream of fire flare up nearby. He went over to investigate, and it was apparent to him from the pattern of the flames that the Chinese below had set fire to a field and expected him to land. He quickly lowered his landing gear because there was precious little fuel remaining, lined up with the flames, and put his airplane down, not knowing where there were holes or rough spots or barriers, artificial or otherwise. To his amazement he hit in a smooth area and the airplane rolled to a stop without incident. When he dismounted, he found himself among friendly Chinese who were overjoyed to see him.

To be lost over wartime China in the black of night was to be really lost. Joe Griffin and our favorite doctor had wandered to the edge of Japanese-held China, and come down in a small village whose airstrip had long since been abandoned as a result of the Japanese advance. Apparently the telephones, if there ever had been any, were also abandoned, which accounted for our failure to get any report of the landing.

How the Chinese realized this was one of our aircraft I will never know, but they are smart people and when they heard the airplane circling overhead they knew the pilot was in trouble. Quick-wittedly, they opened a drum of aviation gasoline from emergency stores and rolled it down the center of the airstrip and then set fire to the spilled gas, forming a more than adequate night-landing system for Griffin's approach. Ray Spritzler and Joe Griffin spent a thankful night with the Chinese. The next morning, after refueling from more of the emergency cache of gasoline, they set out for home.

Looking back, I can distinguish between the foolish and the brave. It is of no use to dwell on how you would behave if you had to do it over because the chance will never come.

I remember John Hampshire for the brave and wonderful man that he was. I remember the doctor who was perhaps even braver in a different way, and how Joe Griffin and the doctor made futile plans to help a good friend who was beyond help. I am proud of these men and their memories, and in spite of our mistakes, I think if we ever had the chance to do it over again, we'd not do it any differently.

Editor's Note: One report said the slug killing John was an American .50 caliber. Somehow, he had passed through the firing pattern of the 75th planes during the melee.

The "Adj"

By Myron D. Levy, St. Louis, Missouri

As "The Adj," I was most fortunate. Virtually all the unit's paperwork was taken care of by a very competent first shirt, sergeant major and clerks. About all I had to do was to sign a few papers now and then. I spent the rest of the time on the flight line, with the pilots and maintenance people, and got to know them quite well.

Although I was not a pilot myself, I was able to share many of their experiences, particularly during their interrogation after they returned from combat missions.

In my judgment, there never has been a fighter squadron as renowned as the 75th. Nor will there ever be again. Those years, the combat in China, the stringent logistical situation, the crummy planes, and a host of other things all go together to make my time with the 75th a period to be treasured in memory.

Some time back, I received a most unusual call from a Colburn Preston, of Vacaville, California. He said he was in the prewar Army Air Corps, stationed at Mitchel Field, on Long Island, New York. Some months prior to World War II, he was assigned to a new outfit formed at Mitchel designated "The 75th Fighter Squadron."

It was sent to Bolling Field, Washington, D. C., then to Baltimore, Maryland, and proceeded from there to India in the very early days of the war. This 75th was en route across India to Burma when a change in orders rerouted it to Alexandria, Egypt, where it was assigned to the 57th Fighter Group, and redesignated either as the 84th or 85th Fighter Squadron. They were part of the Desert Air Force and flew P-40s in support of the British 8th Army, which was fighting Rommel's Afrika Korps.

The squadron later went to Tunisia where it traded it's old, war-weary P-40s for brand-spanking new P-47s. Then the unit went on to Italy, Corsica, Southern France, and Germany, ending up at Stuttgart.

I wonder if the trade-off to P-47s by the erstwhile 75th Fighter Squadron resulted in the 14th Air Force's 75th Fighter Squadron getting the war-weary pieces of junk we did, those old P-40s from Africa.

What finally showed up in China was a batch of beat-up, sad-looking P-40s to replace the even more beat-up P-40s the 75th got from the AVG when it disbanded, as well as the ones our pilots lost during the Japanese campaigns in East China.

These planes were decorated with the grinning Death's Head insignia instead of our familiar Tiger Shark mouths. We were told these P-40s were on shipboard, en route from Europe and Africa to go back to the U. S. A. to be used as scrap, when they were suddenly rerouted to India and thence flown to China for assignment to the 75th Fighter Squadron.

This story adds to The Legend of the 75th. Our squadron, redesignated in Africa, fought against the Nazis as well as against the Japanese Empire.

Most of all, however, I treasure the memories of the guys who were in it. All the other things would have amounted to nothing, but for the people.

I am sure the others in that unit agree with me.

I remember Christmas eve, 1944, at Luliang, China.

And some of the 75th scheming.

Late in November, a senior sergeant at Group HQ phoned and asked me to come over. He said he had some useful information for me.

He felt he owed me a favor because I had gotten his good buddy, Hook Nohel, out of a jam that could have gotten Hook busted before he went home.

I've forgotten the sergeant's name, but his nickname was Mack. He told me that there was to be a ration of good liquor for the rear echelon officers stationed at Luliang.

Unfortunately, there was nothing for the forward element, the combat echelon of the squadron stationed at Chihkiang.

The ration was to be based on the officer head count taken from the unit Day Book of those at Luliang on a certain day in early December. I think it was to be either the 7th or the 8th.

I went back to the 75th Orderly Room tent and went into conference with the first sergeant and the sergeant major.

They prepared records while I only signed them, so they had to be parties to the mischief.

During the last days of November and early December, the 75th Day Book showed officers flying in from Chihkiang daily, and on the target date, we had most of the 75th officers on station "at Luliang."

We had a terrific head count. Over the next several days, we "flew" them all back to Chihkiang.

If anyone had compared the Day Book with the Operations Form 20, I would have been in very deep trouble, because I planned it, and signed off the entries.

Anyway, on Christmas eve, instead of the four or five bottles that would have been correctly issued to the few 75th officers at Luliang, the 75th got several cases. There was Indian Gin (Carew's smooth booze), Argentine Brandy, West Indies Rum and some other genuine alcoholic beverages but no Jing Bao Juice, if you please. Regrettably, there was no Scotch or Bourbon.

There were enough bottles so that all the 75th people at Luliang, both officers and enlisted men, got about half a bottle each.

There was one hell of a 75th party that night.

It was one of the most gratifying nights of my life. About midnight a large group of our people came over to my tent and serenaded me with "For He's a Jolly Good Fellow."

Those are memories!

Saved by a Net

By Don Quigley, Marion, Ohio

The warning net in China saved me one real dark day.

Much of China is without easily identifiable topographical features. Until a pilot learned the territory, getting lost was a real possibility. Helping lost pilots was the Chinese radio-telephone net's second function. Its number one purpose, of course, was to warn our airfields of approaching Japanese fighters and bombers.

When a pilot got lost, rather than flub around trying to find his way home, he would locate a town of some size, then circle it at low altitude and fire his guns in several short, frequent bursts.

Fairly good sized towns usually had a warning net observer who could telephone a message or send one by radio to one of our listening stations. Our people, knowing the location of the town where the message came from, would relay back a message with a compass heading that would lead lost flyers to the nearest friendly area or landing field.

In the 137 missions I flew in East China, I had to use this procedure once. I was leading the 2nd element of four planes in a flight of eight ships under the command of Major Loofbourrow. When he led the flight up through a rather thick overcast, I was unable to find the major's element of four ships after we broke out at the top. I scouted around for a while, changing directions a few times, which turned out to be a mistake, and finally realized we would never get together.

I also realized I didn't know where in hell I was. I didn't want to burn up a lot of gas for nothing, fearing we might run a bit close in getting back. So, I found a break in the clouds and took my four ships down under the overcast. We soon located a fairly large town. I radioed one of the guys in my flight to go down, circle the town very low, and fire his guns. Once he did so, and rejoined, it was a matter of only 10 to 15 minutes before I picked up a call from our station in Changsha, and was instructed to head in a westerly direction. Doing this, dodging clouds as we needed to, we soon came to the river south of Changsha and, of course, were than able to set out course for home, which for us, at that time, was Hengyang.

Thank heaven for our Chinese friends who risked their lives in the Jap-controlled areas of China to man those reporting stations. They knew, as we knew, that if they were caught by the Japs, they would be summarily executed.

Fighting the Japanese took a lot of ingenuity. The Japs learned as the war progressed, the same as we did. And as quickly as we would figure out a way to hit them under unusual circumstances, they would work out a methods of avoiding us. It was a continuous seesaw battle.

When the Japs drove their military trucks during the daylight hours, we gleefully shot up and burned large numbers of them. So they stopped daytime travel. They began moving only at night.

They were driving south along the railroad connecting Hankow in the north to Canton in the south. We were desperate.

As soon as it got daylight, the Japs would pull their trucks off into clumps of trees and camouflage them. By selecting their sites carefully and doing a good job of camouflaging, they pretty well stymied us. Only when they got careless - perhaps, in camouflaging - were we able to locate vehicles by their rectangular shapes. But most of the Jap army trucks were getting through. We needed to figure out something, and fast!

We were flying out of Kweilin where a B-25 squadron was stationed. Lieutenant James Folmar, a member of our squadron, came up with a procedure to help us balance the situation in our favor again. He contacted the guys in this B-25 unit and set up a deal with them to enable us to hit the Japs at night. The B-25s had some high candle-power flares. If they could drop these in areas where we suspected there were Jap vehicles moving, we could go back to work at night, and give the enemy a very bad time.

Here is the way it worked on one night I remember:

After dark, I took a flight of 4 P-40s and followed a B-25 up to just south of our former base at Hengyang. Then I dropped down on the deck and "S'd" the road until I thought I had found a convoy. It was small - 4 to 8 vehicles - because the Japs had wised up and didn't want to risk any more trucks in one location than they thought they could hide effectively. I left my other three fighters at altitude with the B-25, about 3,000 feet above me.

So all could follow where I was, I kept my cockpit dome light on. When I spotted a group of trucks, I would roll back my canopy and fire a Very pistol flare in the air. This was the signal for the '25 to drop a high candlepower flare. He would be following right behind me, and would drop his illuminating flare over the spot where he saw my flare go up.

Then one of my other fighters would drop off while the B-25 and the other two continued following me. The fighter that dropped out would get down on the deck and make about two passes at the trucks, about as many as he could while the light from the B-25's flare lasted. Afterwards, he would head on back to base on his own, his ammunition pretty well gone, and even if it was not, with little chance of being able to catch up with the rest of us anyway.

I'd continue up the road until I found more trucks, and we'd repeat the process. The '25 continued dropping a flare here and there in the hope of seeing trucks which might be trying to escape me. If he found any, he would drop down and strafe with his forward-firing .50s mounted in the ship's nose. We kept this up until all my fighters had a chance to shoot trucks. I'd finish last.

We ran these night missions three times. We were always successful The Japs we caught in moving convoys hated these missions! From the first their truck drivers realized what we were doing. In the light of the flare, we'd see them stop their trucks, hump out of them and run as soon as they saw the first illuminating flare drop from the B-25. They tried to be tricky, too, and keep going at night when things got desperate for them. They'd mask their head-lights, making them so dim and small that we couldn't see them from the air.

But they forgot about their tail lights. These were like red beacons giving us easy targets to strafe, even after the B-25's flare had burned out.

It was incidents like this that illustrated the ingenuity of the American fighting men. We kept coming up with effective ideas when standard procedures were no longer effective. In China, this was doubly important because of the shortages under which we had to operate.

Japs Hit "Our Village"

By Robert T. Smith, Mesa, Arizona

Yunnanyi was "our village." It was a small village in western China, located at the foot of the Himalayan Mountains, 50 miles west of Kunming, the China terminus of the Hump air supply route.

Our village overlooked a small valley with a flat grass field. This was the site chosen by the American Volunteer Group (AVG) as the base for one of its squadrons of P-40s that was designated the 74th after the AVG was disbanded. The squadron's mission was to protect workers and traffic on the Burma Road, and the transports flying the Hump. It was not too far from a beautiful jewel of a lake named Tali. The lake was a fine landmark for returning pilots.

One day a swarm of Japanese fighters and bombers was on us with no warning.

When we first heard them coming and looked up over our shoulders, one guy said, "The B-25s are flying better formation today."

The airfield at Yunnanyi was very primitive. It was only a large rectangular grass pasture. It could, however, accommodate six P-40s taking off simultaneously. Additionally, there was a dirt strip for normal takeoff and landing. In alert, to get as many fighters off as quickly as possible, the grass was used.

Operations was housed in a wooden frame building. It had a ready room for the pilots. In good weather, this room was used mostly to store flying gear.

We in the China Air Task Force (CATF) were used to such "accommodations." CATF had been formed in July 1942 with men who remained behind when the old AVG was disbanded. As the AVG was disbanded, a new unit was activated during combat, and designated the 23rd Fighter Group. One of the squadrons, the 74th, was assigned duty at Yunnanyi and inherited the old AVG's P-40 aircraft.

They were old E-models and nearly worn out. It wasn't until the following March (1943) when they began receiving the newer P-40Ks. Understand, this "new" merely means the first time we ever saw them at the 74th Squadron. The planes themselves were not new from the standpoint of design or usage. Even so, they were a delight to both the pilots and maintenance crews.

Maintenance crews at our village operated from large canvas tents. The P-40s lined up in front of the tents. All maintenance was performed on this flight line. Much of it was at night, or when, for some reason, the planes were stood down. An out-of-commission plane was worked on nearly continuously until it was ready to fly again.

As much as possible, at night, flyable and other aircraft were dispersed at random all over the grass field. We lacked revetments. This dispersal was the best we could do to minimize the planes as targets for Jap air raids. At daybreak, the crew chiefs would taxi the planes back onto the flight line where they would continue to do what routine maintenance they could.

Aircraft fuel was in critically short supply. We often had to limit flying to the most important mission. These included patrols over the Burma Road, and scrambles in response to alerts of possible Jap air attacks. These alerts were known as "Jing-baos."

To avoid using up precious fuel flying patrols over the base for defense, General Chennault developed a radio warning net with Chinese spotters using phones or radios, stationed around the countryside in the form of a grid. When they saw or heard Jap planes, they would phone or radio the information to a central communications center. The message would indicate that "heavy" or "light" engine noise had been heard at a certain grid location on a given heading. With other similar reports from other points on the grid, the central communication center could follow the flight's progress.

When a possible target began to be obvious, the center issued a warning to the base that was threatened. The distance of the enemy planes from the fighter base determined when first alerts were issued. The threatened base would sound an alarm - by turning on a siren or banging on a pan, anything to get the attention of the people there - and one large red ball would be raised on a pole. As the enemy got closer, the second warning was issued, the pan was beaten faster, and a second red ball was raised on the pole.

Now the tempo of the pilot and ground crew activity picked up considerably. Pilots manned their planes. Ground crews were there, ready to assist in starting them. When the third ball went up and the pan was beaten even faster, it meant to get the aircraft into the air as quickly as possible. They were to intercept the enemy planes now known to be coming to hit their base.

It was a very crude system, but effective most of the time. Sometimes, however, the spotters would not hear or see the enemy aircraft. Then the Japs would be on us with no warning.

This happened to the 74th Fighter Squadron at our village of Yunnanyi on 11 July 1943.

The morning began like every other morning. Aircraft were brought back from the dispersal areas and lined up on the flight line. Ground crews relaxed over a cup of coffee in preparation for doing the normal maintenance on their aircraft. The sun was nice and bright. The day was warming.

What a beautiful day until we heard engine noises from the sky. At first, we thought they were friendly B-25s passing overhead.

The flight of aircraft was getting closer to the field. It was now just about over the end of it. Suddenly there was a series of loud booms. We now knew the planes were not B-25s. Someone, rather late, identified them as Jap Betty bombers. There were 20 of them dropping fragmentation bombs on us.

It was too late to get any P-40s airborne. All personnel were running for cover to the slit trenches on the field perimeter. Bombs were walking toward us from the south end of the field, heading right smack toward our flight line.

One sergeant was hit very hard by bomb fragments. A fuel truck exploded. Aircraft were set afire and began exploding. Several men tried to run to the .50 caliber machine gun pits located nearby for base antiaircraft defense. But they were turned back by strafing Jap Zero fighters that had accompanied the bombers.

The Zeros had the skies to themselves that day. They made pass after pass, some so low you could see the Jap pilots' teeth as they smiled, passing us on their strafing runs.

For about 20 minutes, they had a field day. The bombers and Zeros had their fun, did their damage, then departed. Several P-40s were burning and had their landing gear collapsed. We spent several hours putting out the fires. Then we evaluated the damage.

Four aircraft could be made ready to fly that afternoon. They were immediately put on alert status. The refueling truck was unusable, so we had to manhandle 55-gallon drums from the fuel storage dump. We moved them down to the flight line the hard way. We patched the maintenance tents, used hand pumps to refuel the planes from the drums - a very slow process - and did what we could right then to clean up the mess.

Sergeant Brown was the one killed during the raid. His body was removed and our medics treated the injured personnel. Our mascot, a little dog, was also killed. His body disappeared - for burial or for food for some Chinese, we never knew. We had a lot of work to do before we restored a reasonable and capable defense situation. Everyone had to work; the pilots, orderly room personnel, and of course, all maintenance and armament people.

We worked for 24 hours straight, slept when we could, doing our sleeping as well as eating at the flight line. Hardly anyone went to the hostel area. The sheet metal specialists had a great deal of work to do, patching the aircraft skin. Engines and props were changed, using good parts from unflyable planes to restore those that could be put back into flying shape. In effect, we used piles of junk - the wrecked planes - to build flyable ones.

At the end of the fourth day, we had 17 more-or-less flyable ships. We were all very tired, but had a good sense of satisfaction.

After all that work, we were about to relax when we got the message that Kunming was under attack by Jap bombers and fighters. All 17 of our aircraft got off and headed out to intercept the enemy. The 74th fighters caught the Japs over Big Lake and one helluva battle was on. All of us were listening to the radio transmissions from the pilots during the fight. We were with them in spirit.

"I got that SOB!" yelled one.

"Bill, get that one on my right."

And so it went.

Back at Yunnanyi, we were all yelling like a bunch of school kids, rooting for our pilots, to get more kills. Later, we received a report that *none* of the Jap bombers made it back to their home base, and several of their fighters were also shot down.

We had our revenge. Yes, sweet revenge. The squadron was on the way back up again, and the morale was now very high.

Flying Tiger Combat

By Joe Rosbert, Franklin, North Carolina

After a hard day, I could hardly sleep, thinking of the luck it took to get through that kind of combat experience without a scratch.

After picking up our planes that morning at a satellite field named Haig & Haig, we were back at Mingaladon before the sun came up. Just as I was adjusting my Mae West in preparation for a strafing mission at Moulmein, across the Gulf of Martaban, the alarm sounded. Off again to hunt Japs who were still trying to surprise us.

No Japs. After searching the skies in vain, the order over the radio was to proceed to Moulmein on the original mission. A seventh plane joined our flight. It was Dick Rossi.

Heading southeast over the gulf, we were soon approaching an auxiliary airfield about 20 miles south of Moulmein. Since it was so early in the morning and our flight came in low, the Japs had not picked us up on their radio direction finders. It was a disappointment that they had only two planes on the strip. Each of us took a few shots at them while a few men on the ground scampered for cover.

We left the two planes in ruins and headed north for another airfield. The east side of Moulmein was ridged with hills, so we made our initial approach over them directly out of the rising sun. As we came down from the ridge and neared the field, a wonderful sight met our eyes. The Japs had some warning from the pass we had made over their auxiliary field. Some of them were getting into their planes and others were already making their takeoff runs - a pitiful position for them to be in.

We got our planes into single file, and dove on the "sonsabitches." I spotted a Jap at a thousand feet trying to gain altitude. I squeezed the button and, with one spurt from all my six guns, he rolled over and crashed into the hills next to the airport.

There were at least a dozen Japs that got into the air. That, with our seven planes milling around, made for a precarious situation, especially when the big antiaircraft guns began to open up. The puffs of their exploding shells began to appear all around us. They did not seem to have any regard for the safety of their own planes.

When I started to gain altitude in preparation for another pass, I glanced at my fuel supply. I had barely enough gas left to return to base. I advanced the throttle and, at the same time, pushed the nose over to pick up as much speed as possible. Down on the surface of the bay, I streaked for home, rubber-necking for Jap planes the whole way.

Back on the ground, from the accounts of a bunch of excited pilots, I knew we had shot down nine of the Jap planes. That, added to the destruction of the ones parked on the two airfields, made for a very successful morning.

The lunch that was brought out to the field in a Jeep was nothing to brag about. Since the town was becoming more abandoned every day, the mess supervisor had great trouble in obtaining supplies to meet our daily necessities. We had just finished eating the sparse meal when an air raid alarm sounded again.

We managed to get 12 tired planes into the air. I wondered how long our equipment would hold out, with no replacements and no spare parts. The Japs really meant business; there were 54 fighters and 54 bombers! It looked as though this was their supreme effort to knock us out, and the airdrome too.

We were quickly in the thick of another battle. The first Jap I met went into a tight turn, but I had enough speed to pull up sufficiently to lead him for an instant. While I squeezed the gun button, he was blanked out of sight by the long nose of my plane. I pushed the plane over just in time to see him catch fire and head earthward.

Diving on through the fighters, their formation of bombers came into view. I picked the rear one on the right and made a diving quarter attack; but nothing happened; he stayed right in formation. I returned for two more passes. Smoke poured from one of the engines but the plane just would not go down.

Out of the corner of my eye, I spotted a number of Jap fighters approaching to protect the bombers.

I immediately dove down and away.

As it always seemed to happen, when I climbed back to altitude, there was not a plane in sight. After heading east for a few minutes, I detected a speck on the horizon. Closing in, it took the form of a Jap fighter. He was headed home without looking back. At about 250 yards, I squeezed the button and the barrage literally tore off part of his wing. He spun down crazily, crashing into the bay.

Taxiing up to the line after landing, my crew chief, Jake, approached the cockpit. I told him I had shot down two more for sure and two probables. A strange look came over his face.

"What's the matter with your tail?" he asked.

"I didn't know anything was wrong with it," I said.

I looked. Half of my rudder had been shot off. Those Nips had nearly found their mark! I had a weak feeling for a moment.

Jake pulled out some tape and began doing one of his miracle repair jobs as I joined the other pilots in the alert shack. That day we had confirmed 23 Japs with twice that many probables. The First Squadron had also made another record for two days continuous fighting: 44 enemy planes with close to 100 probables.

And all that with only 12 old fighters that could get in the air!

Two Missions

By Edward J. "Smokey" Bollen, Sewickley, Pa.

We were flying cover for some B-24s hitting Hankow. The bombers were coming in at 12,000 feet, and we were at 20,000. It was a nice sunny day, good weather all the way.

On takeoff, I'd had some problem with the coolant system, but I wanted in on this mission bad, so I tried to work it out and not abort. The coolant radiator was in the belly of the ship, in the huge air scoop. The shutters were supposed to open and close automatically to let in as much air as needed to keep the engine temperature normal. If the automatic system failed, you had a cockpit switch for OPEN and CLOSE, so you could more or less control the temperature manually. But it was a lot of trouble and, in combat, you really didn't need that kind of a diversion. But like I said, I wanted on that mission, so I decided not to say anything, but chance it.

We let the bombers finish their run, then escorted them about 20 miles west of the city. There they picked up some P-40s for escorts to bring them the rest of the way home. Us guys in the P-51s turned back and started looking for Jap fighters. Hankow had several airfields, and lots of fighters based there.

We were spoiling for a fight.

Over the city, we started a spiraling descent. Real quick, we started picking up Zeros. The guy on Slocumb's wing had fallen behind so I joined up with him on his wing. He pointed to six Oscars about 3,000 feet below us, about our 9 o'clock position. He nodded and turned in on them from behind. He opened fire much too soon. They saw his tracers and fanned out. I picked the one on the far right. This Jap did a Split-S and went down to 5,000 feet in a steep dive. I got a 90 degree deflection shot at him but I couldn't pull enough to get a lead angle on him. My plane was beginning to buffet and was about to go into a high speed stall.

I knew I couldn't control the coolant system manually in a dogfight. I threw it onto AUTOMATIC and hoped it would work. I was going straight down on the Oscar, shooting. When I went past him, he and his wing man flipped over and went down after me. I kept in a steep dive and pulled out at 10,000 feet with the coolant temperature up against the peg.

I went back to manual control.

There was a huge cloud of smoke from the dock bombing. It went up to about 10,000 feet. I flew into the cloud where I couldn't be attacked, so I could test my engine. I flew around in the cloud on instruments until the coolant system was working again, and the engine temperature down to normal, and with the engine sounding okay to me.

I left the cloud and headed for home. In a few minutes I decided to turn around and go back to Hankow. But at first, I couldn't see any other planes in the air. Then I saw a speck in the sky, due south of me. I was coming up on it from the 7 o'clock position. Somebody got on the radio and told me to waggle my wings. I did, and the speck turned out to be Skip Stanfield. He joined me and we circled over Hankow.

We decided to go down and look at an airfield that was right under us. At 2,000 feet we spotted a Zero and an Oscar going in to land. We fire-walled our throttles and tried to get them before they could set down on the runway. Stan overshot his man on final. I was about a mile behind him and timed my turn so I'd be coming down on the runway just as my man touched down. The set up was perfect. I poured a lot of ammo into him. His plane ground looped off the runway and went into the field.

It was a great mission!

Briefing for the Shanghai strike was on the eve of the attack.

We were expecting to run into a lot of Zeros - about a hundred of them - and we were going up there with only 17 planes from the 75th and another 14 from the 76th. As it turned out, seven of our 31 planes had to abort for engine problems or other difficulties. That left us with only 25 planes on our side.

All the pilots wanted to go, especially a young kid named Little. We got him in the squadron a few months back. He had hurt his hands and Slocumb, the squadron commander, refused to put him on the schedule. Slocumb figured that, since Little was still wearing bandages, this might hamper him when things got rough. He was very disappointed. I could see disappointment on his face as he was standing with the other pilots not on the mission. They were all clustered in front of the alert shack as we cranked up for takeoff. We had a heavy fog early in the morning but, if we had to, we were going to go in spite of it. In his briefing, Slocumb said we were going, regardless.

We all agreed.

It was always easier on your nerves to get the briefing in the morning, just before a mission, then head straight out to your plane and take off. Now, with the briefing last night, the pilots, including myself, lay in bed, unable to go to sleep for a long time, worrying about all the different things that could happen the next day.

For one thing, the mountains were not very far away. In the expected heavy morning fog, pilots would have to take off and climb out on instruments, holding a heading for a certain number of seconds, then do a right turn to a new heading and continue on it until they broke into the open above the weather. This procedure was to keep us in the valley and away from those hard-centered clouds. The climb out would cause me a little sweat until I broke into the clear.

Colonel Ed Rector, Group Commander, had ordered two days of air attacks. He sent the 76th to Kanchow to stage out of that base, along with the 74th. The 118th was to fly from its home base at Suichwan. My 75th would fly out of Chihkiang to Changting, which would be our staging base. Major Slocumb would lead.

The flights would be extremely long. It had taken several days to accumulate enough fuel for the mission.

The next morning, we were surprised to find no fog, only a heavy dew. I was relieved. Our planes were dripping with moisture. All except one which had been painted green were still in their original factory silver. When the green one took off, the runway dust stuck to it and turned it to a kind of brown that the Japanese Zeros used.

We rendezvoused south of Hankow, where the Yangtze River begins its flow from the Tung Ting Ho (lake) to the sea. From there, our attack moved directly eastward over another large lake, Poyang Ho, then on to Shanghai. Colonel Rector ordered one squadron to stay high, for top cover, in case the Japs got any interceptors into the air. He led the other planes against the Japanese fighter bases at Kiangwan and Lungwha airdromes.

At the start of the war, Japanese fighter pilots were superb but combat steadily reduced their original numbers and their training program could not keep up with needed replacements the way the American pilot training program did. The Japs, more and more, were forced to put inexperienced pilots into the air. Their skill level, contrasted with ours, steadily declined.

Many of the Jap pilots based around Shanghai were shot down as they tried to take off to meet our attacks. Our swarm of P-51s made mincemeat of those Japs who did manage to get into the air.

Then we split into four different groups. I went in on the wing of Captain Forrest "Pappy" Parham. The five of us headed for Lungwha, south of Shanghai, on the Yangtze River. I saw Major Slocumb lead his bunch to attack the field on the north side of town. About ten minutes away from our target, Pappy started the descent from 20,000 feet, picking up a lot of speed. About five miles from the airfield, he took two planes down on the deck for strafing. Harper, our Operations Officer, and I stayed up for top cover.

We had come down to about 3,000 feet. I saw some Japs at 12 o'clock, slightly high. Harper and I started to climb. The blinding sun was to the right so we climbed into it to attack the Japs out of it.

As we got close, Harper was on the left. The Jap he was after was heading north and circling to the left. Harper got in behind him and closed. The Jap pilot saw him and started a tight turn. Harper couldn't stay with him. I was farther to the right and in a slight dive, so I turned in on him and hit him when he was about 180 into his turn, and now heading south. I gave him three bursts with a 90 degree deflection. They all hit him. We were using armor-piercing incendiary (API) ammo. When the slugs hit my target, I saw a lot of flashes around the the cockpit and left wing root. These looked like little flashing lights.

I was too close now, and broke it off and started to zoom, using my extra speed to zoom up for altitude. I dropped my left wing to see what the Jap was doing. His left wing had come off at the root and he was beginning to spin. A second later he came out of the cockpit, and his chute opened. Parham later said he saw the guy coming down, but he was just hanging there, looking like he was dead.

Parham and two others made another strafing pass. One of the others was Don King. He and Parham got hit, and turned away from the battle, and bailed out some distance away. From there on, their major concern was to escape, and of course, they had to do it on foot.

Harper and I circled the field. It was clean. We saw one Jap streaking north. It never came back, at least while we were around. Then we spotted a big flying boat sitting in the river. It was right by the airport runway. I knew we couldn't attack it without drawing a lot of defensive fire from the adjacent airport batteries. We both had taken some pretty bad hits anyway, and didn't need any more if we wanted to get back home.

The Japs put a lot of stuff into the air against us that day. I could see tracers above and below me.

Even though Harper had taken some pretty serious hits, since he was leading, he took a sighting on the flying boat and fired - and, luckily, it blew up.

Then we turned up river. Intelligence had told us there was a gasoline dump there. It serviced Jap destroyers and cruisers. It had two big oil storage tanks. When we were still about seven miles out, we began seeing some of the heaviest flak we had seen anywhere. That dump was very heavily defended. We decided it would be suicide for us to go on in, so we turned and flew out. The place should be left to high level bombers.

We flew back to the rendezvous point, about 15 miles south of Shanghai, and circled there with other planes at 20,000 feet, waiting for the remainder to join up. Then I looked down and saw a plane below, rising toward us. It was brown. I thought it was a Zero and dove at it. I was closing when I saw it was John Alerie, flying that dust-covered green P-51. I pulled up alongside of him, and radioed he'd better join up with us because someone else already had made a mistake in identification, and tried to shoot him down.

I took him back to altitude, and he stayed with us.

It was a long, weary, and disheartening trip back to base.

We had scored well against the Japs, but we had our own losses, too, including Parham and our commander, Clyde Slocumb, as well as Don King.

The debriefing was very subdued.

Kitchen Surgery

By Dr. Bob Patterson,
Nashville, Tennessee

Editor's note: This story is a chapter from "Tiger Surgeon," Bob Patterson's book in preparation, and is printed here with his permission.

I was visiting with Tom Tidwell, in his home in Kunming, China, shortly after I was assigned to the 14th Air Force as a Flight Surgeon. Tidwell was a middle-aged American with an obscure, semi-official connection with the Chinese Government.

His most startling features were his penetrating brown eyes and overhung bushy eyebrows. He had a heavy, well-groomed beard. His handshake was firm and his speech brisk. He had been telling me about China and the war situation there when a commotion broke out in the kitchen behind us.

There was a loud banging on the back door.

"Stay where you are!" Tidwell said sharply. "Don't come into the kitchen!" He rushed out of the room and I heard him open the back door. Excited but muffled voices came from the kitchen.

"Major!" Tidwell called. "I need your help."

"Of course," I answered, a bit confused. He had told me not to come to the kitchen for any reason.

A young Chinese lay on the kitchen floor. He was obviously in great pain. His face was half-covered with a towel. Two Chinese coolies stood on each side of him.

Tidwell looked up at me. "Is there anything you can do?" he asked.

I kneeled on the floor and examined the man.

"Have you a knife? A pair of small service tongs?" I asked him. I had identified the leg injury. It was a gunshot wound, superficial, but obviously several days old, and festering.

Tidwell nodded and left the kitchen.

"Get a bottle of whiskey, too!" I called after him.

He came back carrying, to my surprise, a beaten up old leather bag with some crude medical instruments inside it. And a bottle of whiskey. I poured whiskey over the wound area. The limp man on the floor did not flinch although I knew the whiskey must have caused him considerable pain.

Making a bilateral retraction with my hands, I could see a bullet about an inch under the lesion. I sponged the area with my not-too-clean handkerchief soaked in whiskey. Then I removed the bullet with the small tongs I found in the bag.

I poured more whiskey over the area.

"He must go to a hospital at once. He needs more care than I can give him here." I made a circular bandage from one of Tidwell's dish towels, covering the wound.

Tidwell looked at me and shook his head. "Not possible," he said, flatly.

The others in the room eyed me suspiciously. I didn't understand why. Tidwell motioned me to the door.

"Words can't express my gratitude, major," he said. "I very much appreciate your help. More than I can say." I could sense the tension in his voice. "Your ride hasn't come yet, but I must ask you to leave. Please, forgive me. I can't even explain."

I closed the front door myself, and walked down a narrow path toward the small paved road. The Jeep to pick me up was nearly due - according to my watch. I sat down by the roadside and waited. A number of thoughts were going through my mind, none really dominant. I suppose it would be called information clutter. The net effect at the moment was that I felt a mysterious web of China, and realized that it had, somehow, touched me but what was it?

The place where I was sitting was not all that mysterious; just quiet. Of course, I wasn't in "the heart of Kunming." As in most Chinese cities, there was only one well-paved main street. Along it many rickshaws stood waiting in line near all the American-frequented eateries and bars.

At the moment, I would not have minded being in a bar, a real bar. But I had not been in a bar in China yet that didn't serve mainly "jing bao juice." Nowhere could you find Scotch, gin, bourbon, or vodka. A Russian refugee in Kunming did have a distillery where he produced what he called vodka - but it was the weirdest-tasting alcoholic drink I'd ever had. I tried it once and never again.

Near this vodka distillery, several American sergeants were trying to to brew beer. According to reports, it was not nearly as good as the home brew produced back in the States during Prohibition. The effort was a financial failure due to two things: the product didn't sell very well and the owners had too many friends who, like themselves, did a lot of free loading.

The real iniquity, was the city itself, or that part called "slit alley." It was a general term applied to any off-limits place, but specifically, to the area frequented by prostitutes. The colorful name came from the dresses, slit up the sides, worn by the girls of the area.

Chinese streets were not like American ones. Most of the Chinese people we saw seemed to be aimlessly wandering the streets - to our thinking. I wondered where they were going.

But beggars were a different matter. They were always present, in every block. It was a standard practice to give each a few coins. Many had horrible deformities, caused by nature or by accident. Others had been maimed during the war which, for China, had been going on a lot of years before we got into it.

What I missed most in the Chinese streets were automobiles. An occasional car might pass, usually driven by a chauffeur, it's horn making a constant outcry as it wove its way among the rickshaws, walkers, and vendors with partially filled hand carts, carrying fish, garlic, onions, and other produce. The busses were old coal-burning antiques. People packed them inside and hung onto the outside. It was not uncommon for some on the outside to fall to their deaths.

Life in China was cheap.

All Chinese cities had the same stench. It was halfway between the odor of a very old and very over-filled outhouse and the mixture of the rot of people, dead animals, and body odors. It was not a harsh odor, but it was an unseen presence, an enveloping atmosphere, everywhere.

There in the lane beyond Tidwell's house, as I waited for my Jeep, I was letting all this stuff flow through my mind to keep from thinking about what had happened in the kitchen back there. Momentarily, I saw myself as someone like the sawbones of the old Wild West in our country, performing some kind of desperate surgery on a young gunslinger. Shades of those Saturday afternoons at the movies, watching Ken Maynard, Bob Steele and Lash Larue! I smiled at my fantasy, and looked down the street hoping to see my Jeep.

My memory was taking me back to Tidwell's, not to the kitchen, but to the living room - and to the photograph displayed there.

They were the same person! The young man in the photograph and the young man on the kitchen floor were the same.

Or were they? Was I imagining things?

Wheels rattled behind me, and I turned to see a small brown gnome of a man pulling a rickshaw. He stopped, bowed, and smiled. I shook my head and, on second thought, gave him a few coins. He was still smiling broadly and bowing when the Jeep arrived.

Months passed. I was at another base. One day, several Chinese entered my room. One was a soldier I had operated on some months earlier. I had amputated one arm to save his life. Behind him was an interpreter who was saying all the right things. Damn! The interpreter was the young man in Tom Tidwell's photograph, the one on the kitchen floor with a gunshot wound! It was the same individual!

The wounded young man on the kitchen floor had been in Kunming, hundreds of miles from the forward base where I was now stationed with a fighter squadron. How had he gotten here? This "interpreter" was dressed as a coolie, but I knew better.

"How's the leg?" I asked, and immediately wished I'd kept my big Texas mouth shut.

He eyed me coldly. "I beg your pardon?" His English was flawless.

"Sorry," I muttered. "I made a mistake."

From that point on, the interpreting was all downhill, although my one-armed soldier friend kept bowing and smiling.

Several days later the interpreter returned to my office. He came to the point at once. "I can pay you $5,000 American for 1,000 quinine tablets." He kept his voice low, so my medical staff wouldn't hear him.

Dryness tightened my lips. He was working the black market, a clandestine business that was devastating China's economy.

"Get out of here!" I snapped.

He was angry. "All right! But how about 1,000 aspirin tablets for $1,000 American?"

I pushed back my chair and doubled my fists. There was a fine for striking a Chinese but this time, I thought, it would be worth it.

He must have read my thoughts because, in spite of the insulting look he gave me, he turned and stalked out.

I thought no more about him, until about two weeks later, when there he was, facing me in my office again. Fists clenched, I was ready to carry out my threat.

"It's okay, Major. It's okay. He was just doing his job."

It was Chen, one of Tidwell's friends who had come with him, and an associate in a number of unnamed activities. I had met Chen a number of times at Tidwell's following my kitchen surgery. We had become good friends. Chen was not in uniform. He was dressed like a coolie and I had not recognized him. When the surprise and greetings were over, I exploded with all the questions that bothered me.

Before he answered, he checked to see if any of my staff might be within earshot. Satisfied, he said, "Major, this man is Tidwell's son. We're both in Chinese Intelligence. We work side-by-side with Chennault's men in this business."

I looked at young Tidwell. "But why?"

Chen interrupted me. "Major, can you trust everyone on your staff?"

"Yes."

"I guess you know, fortunes can be made by Americans and Chinese in the black market. Drugs are a high priority. No offense, but we have to check everybody. Even you, sir."

I started to ask another question.

Chen closed the subject. "Don't ask. It would be dangerous. If the people dealing in this stuff knew who we really were, they'd gladly kill us. You must be careful. You nearly blew my cover once - the night you came to the hospital. Please, if you see me again under circumstances like this, whatever you do, just don't speak to me. It's not good or safe."

"But where did you come from that night?"

"I work in a lot of places," he answered. "We needed your help that night. We may need it again. We'll contact you when we do."

We talked for a few minutes longer, then they left. Once outside the door, they disappeared into the crowd of coolies who were working on the base.

I expected I would see them again . . . and I did.

Head Hunters

By David J. Brown, Galesburg, Illinois

The Naga head hunters were pretty friendly to our side.

The Japs didn't like them too good because the Nagas had a habit of using Jap heads for interior decorations.

We wanted souvenirs and the Nagas wanted our cigarettes and things, so we were able to do business with them without losing our heads.

One of our men bought a crossbow and a bunch of arrows from a Naga. He sat around in front of the operations shack, fiddling with the bow. He tried firing one of the arrows into the air and it came down between the legs of another boy. It didn't hit him but it came close.

He wasn't too upset until someone told him the Nagas poisoned their arrows.

That was the way the Nagas were able to kill the jackals and other animals so quickly.

From then on, Naga crossbows and arrows were forbidden on the flight line.

One day a bunch of us were sitting on a bench outside the operations shack. One of the guys had a Springfield. After cleaning it, he sat there messing around with it. He passed it around, wanting everyone to look at it so he could brag on the good job of cleaning he'd just done.

Nobody was really interested - cleaning a military rifle wasn't all that much of a thrill. About the time he got his Springfield back, a water buffalo wandered out onto the runway. A small bird was sitting on the buffalo.

"Watch me get that bird!" he said.

He threw a round into the chamber, pulled the rifle against his shoulder and fired.

The buffalo staggered and dropped dead in its tracks. The bird just flew away.

"Whose buffalo was that?" someone asked.

Nobody knew who owned the buffalo. We did know they were domestic animals. Farmers used them for tractors, to pull their plows. We also knew that Uncle Sugar would now have to pay someone for that animal.

If the finance officer could find out who shot it, our man with the Springfield would find the cost of a water buffalo deducted from his next pay. But he didn't.

We also knew we'd have buffalo meat in the mess hall for the next couple of days.

We did.

It was as tough, like old shoe leather.

One day, a transport landed at our base and began off-loading - away from the usual cargo area.

We heard there was something special on board, crates consigned to "COMMANDING OFFICER, 14th AIR FORCE."

The crates were stored in a little building separate from the regular warehouse. We figured that this was a load of hooch for the Old Man.

We hadn't had any good drinking stuff since we left the States, and decided the Old Man wouldn't miss just one little old crate, so we'd lift one for ourselves.

Before beginning the operation, we fortified ourselves with a bit of the local plum wine, to work up our courage. By the time we were well lubricated it was dark, and we thought we were ready. We "quietly" made our way up behind the building where the stuff was stored.

There was a Chinese guard on duty. We knew he had been issued only one round of ammo for his rifle, but none of us wanted it squeezed off in our direction, So we tried to be very careful and silent.

Once inside with the darkness only slightly relieved by the faint illumination from our flashlight, we noticed all the crates had a ripe, red tomato pictured on each end, and wondered what this was for.

We picked up one crate, eased very quietly out the back door with it, and took off for our quarters, happy as pigs in mud, anticipating the pleasure of some real Stateside hooch.

When we pried up the lid and saw the shiny bottles, we found we'd liberated a case of catsup.

We had a heavy bomb outfit on the other side of the field. These guys dug a cave out of the side of a hill and put in a sort of a restaurant where you could order an omelet or something else, and a counter where you could sit and eat it.

They also had a latrine close by, in case you got hit with an attack of GIs while eating, something that did happen now and then, as their eggs were no more guaranteed fresh than ours.

That outfit was pretty good, though. They got some food in India and ferried it up in their ships. There was no other way to get Stateside food in China except to bring it in yourself.

All regular chow was provided by the Chinese Government War Area Service Command. The combat needs of the 14th Air Force took all the Hump tonnage available, leaving nothing for such incidentals as food.

On the whole, this outfit across the field from us ate a whole lot better than we did, but we didn't gripe too much, as long as they let us eat in their cave-restaurant. Their prices weren't bad, either.

Sometimes we'd get pretty PO'd when we saw what ATC was ferrying up, especially when we wanted American food so badly. Some of the fancy stuff that was off-loaded from the cargo ships ticked us off; stuff like desks, chairs and file cabinets for some "chair-borne commandos." These clowns just had to have their equipment so they could write their useless reports and send them off to the Theater Headquarters in New Delhi, India.

Our pilots tried to help us whenever they went on a trip to India, by bringing back as much as they could stuff into the cracks and crannies of the planes they ferried. But this wasn't much, until one of them got an idea. He took a crash ax and cut a trap door into a 75-gallon belly tank, leaving one side intact as a hinge. The pilots going to India would take this with them. When they came back, they had it filled with goodies for us. It was a bit ragged about the edges, but the pilots were careful, and none got scratched or cut.

Before a pilot left for India, we would take up a collection and get a list from each guy as to what he wanted. He'd bring back what he could get from the PXs in India. Sometimes, he'd drop the ammo out of his ammunition trays in the wings, and load them with goodies, too. We really appreciated this.

With black market prices what they were, $25 for a five-pound can of SPAM, toothpaste $5 a tube, and American whiskey for astronomical sums, the black market was simply beyond us.

Our pilots made life a little bit easier for us when they brought this stuff back, and for PX prices, too. It didn't please the black market operators very much.

Local Rice Flailer

By Oswin "Moose" Elker, Rochester, Minnesota

On 29 July 1944, we were returning from a strafing mission to Sintsiang. We passed close to Siangtan Air Field which had recently been occupied by the Japs. I spotted some planes on the field and took the low flight of four planes down to strafe.

In order to get at the targets from our position we had to fly right between two rows of double story barracks. When we did, the windows lit up with gun fire like Fourth of July sparklers. My first target turned out to be a decoy plane, so I switched my gunfire to a shop building behind the decoy. It caught fire.

Since I had been firing my guns, I did not notice the hits on my plane. Lopez, who was leading our top cover flight, called out that someone in the low flight was streaming coolant. A quick glance at my engine temperature gauge told me that it was me!

On our last strafing run, we were heading east, so I made an immediate 180 to the west toward a more hilly and less accessible area. We were in enemy territory, and I wanted to put as much distance between those people and me as I could before leaving my ship.

As my engine temperature continued to climb the engine began to detonate. I reduced my power setting, dropping the manifold pressure, and was able to get the engine to smooth out somewhat. I was still trying to get as far from that Jap airfield and its adjacent town as possible. The engine temperature kept rising rapidly, so I had to continue reducing my power setting. I fell so low I could no longer maintain flying speed except by sacrificing some of my 1,500 feet of altitude.

At this point, I trimmed the controls to hold the plane in a stable attitude, headed in a northerly direction, and bailed out.

I landed on the side of a steep hill, about 200 yards from a farmer's house. The people there quickly took me in, and gathered my chute, burning it to erase any trace of my presence. Inside, they immediately shaved my head and cut off my reddish-colored mustache, then outfitted me with the familiar light blue coat and pants of the

Chinese laborer, complete with the conical coolie hat. Then they hustled me farther back in the hills till we reached another farm house. Now, it was just about dark.

I didn't get much sleep that night. It seemed that everytime I dozed off, they were shaking me awake to move me farther back into the hills.

The guerrillas, who had joined our group, heard of a Jap patrol coming toward our location.

We spent most of the night stumbling over rocks and brush, going either up or down hill. It seemed there was no flat land. I really didn't believe we were in any great danger of being overtaken as any search party coming after us would have to cover the same rough terrain we were contending with. Since there were only foot paths, there was no faster means of transportation they could use to try and catch us. We moved on our feet, and they would have to do the same.

We traveled west all the next day, then rested one day at still another farm house. The third day we felt quite confident, so we made our way to a flagstone road that was wide enough for a two-wheel cart. This prompted our leader to get a "sedan chair" for me. However, this bore only a very slight resemblance to the ones I'd seen in the movies. It had no overhead canopy, and the bamboo poles for carrying it were far from being a matched set. The left one was about 2-1/2 inches in diameter, while the one on the right was only about 1-1/2 inches. The right one bowed under my weight and gave the chair a definite list to the starboard.

To prevent the risk of inflicting permanent curvature of my spine, I convinced them that I would rather walk. However, it seemed that they felt they were losing face by letting me walk, so whenever we came within sight of a settlement, I had to ride again. During these face-saving rides I kept wishing the sedan chair had trim tabs so I could make it "fly level" for me.

We had been on the road heading west about half a day when we were overtaken by a young man. He arrived on a dead run, all out of breath, and excitedly pointing to our back trail. Between gasps for breaths, he was trying to tell the guerrillas something. They quickly looked in all directions for an alternate course. However, we were in a small flat valley with no nearby physical features behind which we could take cover.

After some shouting and what sounded like excited arguing, they hustled me up a path 90 degrees to the road, north about 150 yards, to an area where some men and women were flailing rice. There were no protective buildings, just a flat, open, hard-packed area for threshing grain.

They grabbed one of the women and put her in the sedan chair, and handed me her flail. From our traveling group, four quickly carried the chair with the lady in it down to the cart path, and headed in the direction we had been going before the interruption. With my garb, I blended completely with the group of rice flailers.

Keeping me briefed on what was happening did not seem to rate very high on their agenda. By this time, I was thoroughly confused, and more than a little apprehensive.

I was given a crash-course in rice flailing in several Chinese dialects in loud, high-pitched voices. They were all very excited. Of course, no matter how loud they hollered, I understood none of it.

From Rev. Tomig, one of the missionaries near where I was stationed, I had learned how to count in Chinese, so after some repetition and finger pointing around the circle of rice flailers, I figured out that I was number five.

As the chief honcho counted from one to eight, the individual with the corresponding number was to strike the pile of rice with his flail. To give this dumb American who didn't even know how to flail rice, a chance to catch on, the counter started at a rather slow pace.

The four men carried the lady in the sedan chair down the path at a very leisurely pace. They even stopped occasionally, I supposed, to show the pursuing group that they weren't running away; that indeed, they were not even in any hurry. At first, I did not understand this, but later realized they also did not want to get out of sight of me until they had been spotted by whoever it was following our back trail.

At the sight of a small group of men approaching, they picked up their pace some.

The sight of the approaching men also prompted our honcho to increase the tempo of his counting, I supposed, to make the operation seem more realistic. As our honcho counted, "Ee, Er, San, Sah, Woo . . ." at my number, I gave the rice pile a good whack. But in the mounting excitement I yanked my flail back much faster than necessary. As a result a piece of board at the end of the leather flail caught the "Sah," or number four man, neatly across the shins.

I got an unsolicited course in advanced Chinese swearing. I don't know exactly what he said but, based on the apoplectic look on his face, I'm sure it must have included all his major and minor deities, my ancestry for several generations back and, quite likely, most bodily functions!

I remembered the Chinese word for "excuse me," which I said over and over again to this man. It only brought more outbursts from him. So I took my place in the circle again, and we made a few more rounds with the flails, without the number four man in the circle. During this humiliating fracas, the small group of pursuing men on the the road caught sight of the sedan chair in the distance, and broke into a run to overtake it.

Then, just as suddenly as I had been thrust into the production line, I was yanked out. As soon as the running men had disappeared around a bend in the road, still in hot pursuit of the sedan chair, my remaining escorts and I headed over the hills on the run.

Up to this time, the Chinese had not bothered to give me any explanation of our rice flailing charade. I strongly suspected the group of men following us on the road were Japanese. Later, I verified this. The patrol must have had some very definite information as to what was supposed to be in the sedan chair. As a result they paid scant attention to the rice flailers. Rice flailers at this time of the year were a common sight in this valley.

I thought that when we once got away from the threshing bee, my embarrassment over hitting the man with my flail would end. But my guerrilla friends would look at each other, then at me, and slap their shins and burst out laughing. Equally funny to them was pantomiming how the patrol chased the sedan chair. The bright spot for me was that we were rid of the lopsided sedan chair!

I very much appreciated this seemingly light-hearted behavior, especially in the face of the fact that these people who were helping me would most certainly have been summarily shot were they caught.

The Chinese had supplied me with sandals along with the rest of my clothing disguise. I could walk very comfortably with them, although I would have preferred a more leisurely pace. To my continued embarrassment the hilarity did not end when they turned me over to a new group who were to continue to guide me on my way. I soon understood that all the details of the rice flailing incident had been retold, along with all the gestures and profanity that had accompanied it, probably embellished a bit with each repetition.

After another week of walking we came to a town that had a Catholic mission. This was well within friendly territory, so it also had some kind of an airfield. At the mission, I learned that Rosie (Rosenbaum) had been there for several days and was waiting for a plane to pick him up. Presently the plane came and took us both to Kweilin. I had called ahead from the mission, to let our squadron know that I was okay and coming in.

This was the first news that they had received of me. As a joke, Flash Segura conspired with the others to have all my belongings distributed to various members of the squadron. Soon after I entered my completely denuded bunk space, the squadron members dropped by, one by one, or two at a time, wearing various articles of my clothing. They made remarks like, "Gee, Moose, we didn't think you'd need these anymore," or "Hell, we all thought you were dead." Whereupon they'd peel off my article of clothing and toss it onto my bunk with an air of reluctance.

Bill Carlton gave quite a performance, as if he wasn't going to give me my shoes back since they fit him so well. Walter Daniels said that he thought it was pretty cheap of me to want my clothes back.

They had a lot of fun at my expense, but I didn't care. I was glad to be back.

Doc Laughlin called me into his little hospital to check me over. In the process, he asked me some thinly disguised psychiatry-type questions.

Then he asked me to recount my experiences in getting out of enemy territory. I barely got to the point where I bailed out, when he completely took over the conversation, recounting an endless series of incidents where he had narrowly escaped detection by the dean of his medical school for some prank he had pulled while a student there. I was beginning to suspect that I was supposed to feel mighty fortunate that I had merely been shot down by the Japs rather than having been required to endure the greater risks at his medical school.

When he finally ran down, he said he was grounding me temporarily while he assessed my physical condition and evaluated our (mostly his) conversation.

My encounter with Doc Laughlin brought to mind Colonel Loofbourrow's visit to the doc for a cold or some minor sore throat ailment. This was when the CO had first joined the squadron. Upon emerging from the dispensary 45 minutes later, Phil Loofbourrow said, "Well, I guess I'll never have to go see him again; he told me everything he knows!"

After escaping from Doc Laughlin, Captain Glass called me in for a debriefing. He already had all the information concerning our strafing run from the other seven members of the mission. Now he was looking for any significant military information I might have picked up while behind enemy lines. I told him all I learned was that the Japs built some fairly realistic decoy planes, that our P-40s would not fly very long without coolant and that a person could lose 15 pounds in two weeks by running up and down hills in the dark, while trying to subsist on a diet of rice and *eggis*! I didn't tell him about my rice-flailing lesson, though.

Since this was the second time I'd returned from a mission on foot, Colonel Loofbourrow put the icing on the cake when he asked me: "'Moose,' whose side are you on?"

I didn't mind. I was too glad to get back - a second time.

Fireball in the Night

By George E. Hibarger (dec)

We were a long way from all our China fighter units, sitting behind Jap lines, having to operate entirely from supplies airlifted in. The Japs had taken the Central Valley the past summer.

This thing happened one night early in 1945 at Suichwan where I was stationed with the 118th Tac Recon Squadron. Just past the new year, we got a couple of Northrop P-61 night fighters assigned for base defense. They were called Black Widows. They were big planes with two R-2800 P&W engines to move them along. They carried a crew of two, a pilot and a second guy they called a radar operator. Most of us had only the faintest notion of what radar was or what it could do.

These ships were to protect us against Jap raids during the night and in bad weather. But they didn't get a lot of business. By the time, the P-61s got there, the Japs had about stopped hitting us after dark.

One night, with nothing to do, I decided to visit a guy I knew who worked in Fighter Control. I borrowed the operations Jeep and drove up there, using headlights because we were not under any alert condition at the time.

I had hardly arrived, when the alert sounded. It was a 1-ball. A couple of minutes later, the 2-ball sounded, however. We weren't far from the runway, so I could hear the P-61 engines start up. The Black Widow night fighter was soon in the air. Inside the tent with the fighter control guy whom I was visiting, I heard the pilot check in on the radio.

The weather was cruddy. The overcast dipped below the tops of some of the hills in the area, but the P-61 pilot wasn't worried. He had both a radar operator on his plane and fighter control on the ground to help him. Even as primitive as radar was at that time, he figured it was sufficient to get him back in. I stood behind the controller while he worked the night fighter who had found a target, an unknown.

Control directed the P-61 to intercept it.

I felt funny about it. I asked control if he was sure that it was a Jap plane, and he told me that since the first alert sounded, all American planes had been warned to stay away from the area because of a possible hostile. The Black Widow's target was the only plane that had not paid heed to his instructions. His orders were quite clear: "Shoot down any unresponding planes!"

The target airplane seemed to be just stooging around, flying first in one direction, then another. This was common with Jap bombers when they hit a base at night with a single plane. It took some time for the controller to get the P-61 into a position to make contact with its own on-board radar, but finally the radar operator reported a contact. He took over control from fighter control, and continued to direct his pilot to close on the plane.

In a few minutes, the pilot called a "Tally-ho!" He closed to try and make a visual identification. He had to get in pretty close because of the scudding clouds at his flight level.

"Hey, Control, this looks like a B-24," he called. "What'll I do?"

"There are no American planes in your area. Blow it out of the sky."

"Wilco. Here goes."

A moment later, the pilot came back on the air, his voice high-pitched with excitement. "Man, oh, man. I don't know what he was carrying, but when my 'twenties hit, it made one great big explosion and fireball. We had to fly through some of the stuff."

"Roger. Return to base." The controller gave the pilot a heading. The P-61 started back, landing about 30 minutes later. The controller completed his log. A few minutes after that, at the end of his shift, I drove him back to our living area.

It was a week or so later, the Chinese brought in a very poor specimen, an American, badly beaten up and with some serious burns. It turned out that he was the navigator on a B-24 tanker, inbound to Suichwan, that got lost. Its radios were inoperative and his crew had been unable to call for help or receive the warning to vacate the area.

Our BlackWidow night fighter had suddenly turned the navigator's plane into a hot fireball. He couldn't remember how he got out. The first thing he remembered was floating down under his chute - the only survivor.

I Hit a Pagoda

By Dave Rust, Houston, Texas

I was not proud of the pagoda incident and I have never told the whole story until now. It happened on the morning of 2 June 1944. Paul Moerning and I were on standby. Both of us had in-commission airplanes. Mine had just come out of a wing change. The squadron was off on a mission, and a 1-ball sounded.

We didn't worry about it because we'd been getting a lot of 1-ball scares. Pretty soon this one went to a 2-ball. Paul and I scrambled. I got my bird started first, so I took the lead on takeoff.

Takeoff was north. I started a slow left turn but my airspeed was reading low, probably from rain in the pilot tube. I dropped the nose just a bit to be sure - but something warned me: *pagoda! pagoda!*

At that instant, I hit the pagoda.

My left turn was just enough to keep the pagoda hidden under my nose. I saw the blur, and felt the shock as I hit the stone spire with my right wing. There I was, upside down in a very crippled airplane, and not very high off the ground.

My first conscious thought was to get the power on that bird. By the time the command got to my throttle hand, the engine was already wide open. My fighter pilot reflexes were there ahead of my brain. The engine torque plus full stick rolled me upright, and I was able to hold it right side up, though only with great effort. I thought the flaps ought to even things up a bit, and they did, enough that I was no longer worried about climbing high enough to bail out.

When I got a couple of thousand feet, I thought it over and decided to have a go at landing it. I knew I could hold it level at 140. Besides, there was the problem of getting out of a plane that would certainly go into violent rolls as soon as I released the stick. I came in tail-high, and spiked it on the center strip between the runway and taxiway, just in case I blew it. But it went perfectly.

I taxied in, wishing I didn't have to.

I was going to take the plane directly to the engineering shed. But Phil Loofbourrow stopped me as I was taxiing by operations. All he said was, "Didn't you know the pagoda was there?" That was bad enough, but the expressions on those mechanics' faces were worse.

They had just spent a month changing that wing, and I had destroyed all their work in a split second.

All that would have been over in a day or two, but then came the word about the kids. The report said when I hit the pagoda, it was full of kids from a nearby school. One child had been killed and two others badly hurt. I just wasn't able to handle that. I was a 19-year old kid with a lot of insecurity, except in the cockpit of a plane. I hated what I had done, but couldn't find the right response. Any response would have been better than what I did, which was nothing. I know now that Loofbourrow or P. C. Wen, or many of the others could have straightened me out, but I was too scared of showing weakness to ask.

The war went on but I couldn't forget about it.

The reason I never told the story was not simply an effort to cover up a dumb stunt. The North Pagoda at Hengyang was, like many, used as a Ching Pao shelter. I didn't have to think about it.

Until I experienced the forgiving grace of Jesus Christ, in 1973, it was good that I didn't think about it. There was no turning back the clock, and nothing to be done to even partly express my regrets and compassion to the children' parents. The thing was buried so deep that even when comrades innocently joshed my mind about it, I couldn't explain why it wasn't a joking matter.

Only after I learned the truth recently did I realize that I no longer had to live with that feeling of guilt. In truth, I am finally free of it, free from the guilt of the accident and the guilt of my failure to act like a man and do what I could for the families of those children.

Editor's Note: Myron Levy, the unit's adjutant when the event happened, said this:

"I got very upset when I received the above letter from Dave Rust, because I KNEW he had been deceived about the death and injuries of the children. As the Adjutant, I was responsible for liaison with the City of Hengyang through my counterpart in town, Mr. P. C. Wen. I was made aware of all happenings that affected the relationship between the Chinese and the squadron.

"There were no casualties as a result of Dave Rust hitting the Pagoda. I called Phil Loofbourrow, our C. O. at the time, and related the contents of Dave's letter to him. He confirmed that there were no casualties. Phil also said that the construction of the pagoda was such that the spire could not have injured anyone inside, if in fact, there was anyone in it at the time.

"By coincidence, Flash Segura called me with a Cajun story and I related the matter to him. He stated that he had personal knowledge of the incident, that he saw the accident and knew there were no casualties.

"I called Dave and told him that he had been the victim of a false story, a cruel practical joke. I am incensed that he had to carry this load of guilt around for all these years. Fortunately, he was able to cope with it, and in time, to be free of it."

A Taste of Combat

By Don Van Cleve, Irving, Texas

It was in the spring of 1944. I was assigned to the 75th Fighter Squadron and stationed at Hengyang. We were being pressed real hard by the Japs, and our pilots were flying a lot of missions each day. It was hard on them, and just as hard on our P-40s, too. The shark mouths painted on the cowls of the planes may have looked pretty fierce to the Japs, especially if they were seeing them nose-to-nose, with those six 'fifties converging on them. But the paint job didn't make the planes go any faster, and it didn't keep them from breaking down a lot, and more so, since many of our planes were old, weary and just plain worn out.

I was a crew chief; I knew!

One day our maintenance officer sent for me. He said that "Vurgie," one of our pilots, a Lieutenant Vurgaropoulus, was down at Changsha, about 100 miles north of Hengyang. He had a damaged fuel line. The MO was sending me there to do the repair. I wasn't happy with the prospect of a torturous trip by Chinese train and truck.

I knew from hard experience that 100 miles on the Chinese transportation system would be an all-day trip, and a very uncomfortable one at that. I'd made other trips before, always glad I didn't have any loose teeth: I'd lost 'em for sure! Outside the large towns and cities, most Chinese roads were not much more than a pair of ruts. By the time we reached Changsha, I felt like we had made twice the mileage up-and-down as we did going forward. When it could feel anything, my can felt the same way.

Anyway, the trip took me eight hours. A few minutes after getting used to being on firm ground again, it didn't take me much time to fix the damaged fuel line. Lieutenant Vurgaropolus leaned into the cockpit as I sat there running up the engine and checking it out to be sure we were getting proper fuel pressure, and that the engine was delivering full power.

After shutting down and giving the engine some time to cool, I checked for sign of fuel leaks, all the way back well beyond where the line had been damaged, to the firewall. When I was satisfied, I replaced the cowling and tightened the Dzus fasteners holding it in place.

"All yours, Lieutenant."

"Okay, Don. Running good and no leaks?"

He knew there were no leaks. He knew I wouldn't have given him his plane back if I had any doubts.

I just nodded. The "sirring" and formal address by rank and grade was not very popular in the China combat outfits. When it was used, it was more of a nickname variety than observance of military discipline. The pilots all knew they wouldn't get off the ground without the support of all the ground personnel. They appreciated what we had to go through to keep these wrecks flying. Besides, most of us crewing the planes were older than the pilots flying them, and I think they gave us the respect of our age difference. There was a much closer and more friendly relationship between the enlisted men and the officers in the Air Corps than in the other branches of service. Most of us thought this helped, rather than hurt our combat effectiveness.

"How soon are you going back, Don?"

"Right away. I don't want to spend the night here. The truck will take me back to the station, and I'll catch the next train south."

"How long will you have to wait?"

"Dunno. They don't keep schedules. Might be here all night."

"Hate to see you go through that again. You looked beat when you got here."

"I *was* beat."

"It's only 25 minutes to Hengyang by my P-40. How'd you like to ride back with me?"

Man, was I ever agreeable to that idea! But I didn't know how we could pull it off. The 'forty was designed for only one guy - the pilot - to ride in it. I nodded anyway.

"Look, let's put my chute and your tool box in the baggage compartment, and you ride in the cockpit with me, taking the space where the chute usually is. I'll sit on your lap, and in a few minutes, we'll be home. It ought to beat another long train ride."

"What if you need your chute?"

"You fixed the plane, didn't you? I doubt I'll need the chute."

"Well, how about when we get back, and you get another mission, but we find something in the baggage compartment has spilled on your chute on the trip, and it has to go to repack?"

"No sweat; I'll use a spare, or borrow somebody else's."

It sounded good to me. After getting Vurgie's chute and my tool box tucked into the baggage compartment and secured as best I could, I got into the cockpit, and loosened the seat belt and shoulder harness so it would fit around both of us.

When I was settled, Vurgie got in and sat on my lap. I was thicker than the chute he normally sat on, so he kicked the rudder adjustments to bring the pedals back a notch, moving his feet back, but still allowing him to get full rudder movement. Once he was strapped in, he started the big Allison engine. After a couple of coughs and puffs of blue smoke out the exhaust stacks, it held. Vurgie ran the mixture control up to full rich. He gave the gauges a quick check, then popped his thumbs outward, and one of the guys on the ground pulled what passed for wheel chocks. We started taxiing out to takeoff position.

It didn't take us a minute to get to the downwind end of the runway. Here he quickly turned the P-40 into the wind, and did the run-up. The mags checked okay, so he closed the canopy, rolling it forward and locking it in place. Then he turned the plane and eased it into takeoff position. After another quick check of his instruments, he shoved the throttle forward against the stops. The familiar roar of the engine blocked out everything.

As a crew chief, I had run up 'forties, but I hadn't flown in one before, as we didn't have any two-place ships in our squadron. I was startled how fast the plane seemed to gain speed. With the tail down, I couldn't see anything, but in a few seconds, the pilot shoved the stick forward, then popped the tail up off the ground. I felt better, being able to see where we were going now. Just past the middle of the runway, we were airborne.

Vurgie brought back the prop pitch control to the climb RPM even while the gear was still retracting. Then he came back on the throttle some, to climb power, but we were still pulling a lot of inches of manifold pressure. He was smooth.

The ground dropped away quickly. Vurgie turned west, and we were soon out over the lake, over Tung Ting Ho.

"Hey Don, look," he shouted. I could barely hear him over the engine's roar. He pointed down. "That's a Jap ferry down there."

I nodded.

"Don, how'd you like to get a combat mission?"

I nodded again, hard, and grinned too.

Vurgie adjusted his power settings, gave the instruments another scan, made a quick but careful sweep of the sky for possible Jap fighters, then dropped his left wing and shoved the nose of the P-40 down. Airspeed picked up quickly. Vurgie flipped up the guard covering his armament switch for the guns, without looking away from the target. We were hitting close to 300 when he leveled off just above the water. Then he opened up with those 'fifties. Man oh man, was I ever glad I wasn't in that boat! What a job those six fifty-caliber Browning machine guns did, especially at their point of convergence! Vurgie chopped that boat in two.

Some of the passengers jumped overboard when they saw us coming, but most of them were knocked overboard by the slugs from the 'fifties. The entire firing pass didn't last more than a few seconds, but the Japs would have to get them a new ferry and a bunch of replacements to ride on it.

What a mess! After we passed over it, Vurgie hauled up the plane's nose and dropped his left wing as we climbed back to altitude. He looked over his shoulder to see what damage had been done, he also made a quick, twisting search of the sky. No point in getting surprised by Jap fighters while checking what we had done to the ferry and its passengers.

The water was littered with debris, various sized chunks of the boat, bodies, water reddened with their blood. I shivered thinking I understood a little bit better why the Japs hated those shark-mouthed P-40s so much, especially ours. They could always pick them out because of the white prop spinners that identified the 75th's planes. Our ships were on them daily.

They hated us with a passion.

For me, what a thrill!

The flight back to Hengyang took 25 minutes, just as Vurgie said it would. We hit the traffic pattern. Vurgie bent it around, jamming me hard into the seat, and nearly blacking me out. At the top of his widow-maker pattern, he dropped his landing gear. In a few seconds, I felt them thump into place, with the popups showing above them, on each wing. As we turned final, he put the flaps down. I felt the plane try to act like an elevator with the added lift. He watched the ground closely, and slowly reduced his speed, lifting the nose until we were in a 3-point attitude, but real close to the ground. Then as the speed bled off, the gear touched the runway, a little bumpy, but with no bounce.

A good landing.

Vurgie turned off the runway, and taxied up to the line of other P-40s, then shut down. As soon as the prop stopped, he put the ignition switch to off, unbuckled the harness, and pushed against me to get out. It made me sweat some, even though he had opened the canopy while we were taxiing back in. He stood on the wing and filled out the forms.

"How about that, Don? A 25-minute combat mission. Ops'll love that!"

"Yeah." But my mind wasn't on that. I had lost all feeling in my legs and feet and couldn't get up.

"Need some help to get out?"

"Nah." I wasn't about to admit that I couldn't handle it myself. Using my hands, I pulled my legs up, knees cocked, getting relief from the pressure of the seat edge, and rubbed my legs to get the circulation going again. It was 10 minutes before I could get out of the cockpit. Vurgie was gone by then, into operations, to report the flight. I walked carefully over to the maintenance area. Several of the other crew chiefs came out to meet me.

"Hey, Don, is that right? You really get a combat mission?"

I nodded and grinned. Man, was I ever proud!

The Phantom P-40

By Wallace Little, Fort Walton, Florida

Part of this story is like unconfirmed legend - intriguing and hard to prove. What made it so special was that it involved John Hampshire in the end.

Hampshire was a legendary fighter pilot. Many say he was the greatest who ever flew.

I heard tantalizing portions of the "phantom" when I was first assigned to the 75th Fighter Squadron in 1944 - about a year after Hampshire's death. In the years since, I've picked up occasional comments on it, mostly from those who served the 14th Air Force or attached units in China during World War II, or from others who had some other personal interest in the air war in China.

Until recently, I had little success in confirming any portion of it. Even now, much of it still remains simply a fascinating legend.

The fact remains that the story's details are accurate enough to make total fabrication of such a tale seem unlikely.

The story began early in the war on Mindanao, the southern-most large Philippine island. The U.S. forces there had been defeated by the Japs. Our Army Air Corps planes, fighters, and others had been wiped out by the Imperial Japanese Air Force.

One miraculous exception was a single P-40, an early model. It had been assigned to the Philippines in the years prior to WWII and still carried the old Air Corps star-and-red ball insignia. It was in pretty bad shape. Those Americans who were there kept it carefully hidden from the nearly daily Jap recon flights. This group of Americans included several aircraft mechanics and one lone pilot. Using parts cannibalized from other wrecked P-40s, they began rebuilding this one.

From the various details I've accumulated, at least this portion of the legend appears to be true.

They could not reconstruct the P-40's landing gear so they rigged up a set of bamboo skids and fastened them in place. They were rigged so they could be dropped, once the plane was in the air. In time, all the repairs that were possible had been made.

The lone pilot who had survived the defeat wanted to take one more crack at the Japs. The Americans scrounged the other wrecks, and come up some bombs and with enough ammunition to load the guns. They also found enough fuel to fill the P-40's tanks, including the fish-glued bamboo drop tank they made to extend the old P-40's range.

The pilot decided the best chance would be to fly to Formosa, a distance of 1,000 miles, most of it over water, and hit the Japs there. He rightly concluded that the Japs would not expect such an attack. The P-40 could probably sneak in and do its worst damage to one of the Jap airfields there. Afterwards, the pilot would fly to China, and crash-land at one of the AVG Flying Tiger bases.

Just before takeoff, the Americans cut a narrow runway through the cogon grass and brush, using machetes and their bare hands.

It was just wide enough to handle the P-40 on its strange looking skids, and was barely long enough to accommodate a takeoff run.

The pilot buckled himself into the cockpit, waved to his pals and started the engine. Once it had settled down, he managed to make a scary takeoff, dropping the improvised bamboo skids, once he was safely airborne.

He set his course for Formosa. According to the legend, the P-40 reached its target, catching the Japanese on Formosa completely by surprise. The pilot dropped his bombs, and strafed until he ran out of ammunition, doing considerable damage to the Japs. Then he hit the deck and headed west over the water for mainland China.

At Kweilin, an American air base in the China central valley, a unit of the China Air Task Force, the 75th Fighter Squadron, was operating against the Japs with considerable success. As evening approached, the Chinese radio warning net reported a single unidentified plane approaching. It appeared to be headed for Kweilin.

Two pilots, Hampshire and Costello, were scrambled. They jumped into their P-40s and took off, climbing to intercept the unknown plane. When they found it, their identification was difficult because of the fading light and the apparent meat-ball insignia on its fuselage. It looked like a strange Jap plane, but the insignia didn't look like it was American either. They tried to contact it by radio, but were unable to do so. They tried to shoot it down. It offered no resistance, nor did it take any evasive action: it simply continued on its straight and level flight, as if it had been trimmed for this and was flying on autopilot, except that P-40s were not equipped with autopilots.

Hampshire and Costello nearly shot the old plane to pieces, but they were unable to knock it down. After they ran out of ammunition, they followed the old plane until it ran out of fuel. They watched it crash into a rice paddy and burn. Then they returned to Kweilin.

Investigators who later found the wreckage, identified the plane as an early model American P-40. From charred fragments of documents on the body of the pilot, they identified him as American.

At that time, Jim Shannan was a C-47 copilot. He was flying with a Colonel Wayne K. Richardson. They were to fly from Kweilin to Kunming late that afternoon. He saw Hampshire and Costello take off for the interception, then return about dark, reporting a kill.

I talked by phone with Lorin Miller, who was Hampshire's crew chief at the time of the interception. Although he now has difficulty speaking, he said that Hampshire returned from that mission saying he had fired on a "different-looking" Jap fighter plane that had offered no resistance, but he had been unable to shoot it down. After using up all his ammunition, he had followed the plane until he saw it crash and burn.

Neither Hampshire nor Costello ever discussed the interception other than at the regular combat debriefing. Other pilots who have flown the P-40, including myself, wonder, if the story is true, how the P-40 was able to fly straight and level with no one on the controls. It was not that stable in a hands-off condition. It would have started a spiral either to the left or the right if left unattended for even a relatively short period of time.

Even so, the story is widely told, even at this late date. One I cannot help but wonder if it is not wholly or at least partly true.

Overshot Landing

By Don Van Cleve, Irving, Texas

In the summer of 1944, a 75th fighter pilot named Oswin "Moose" Elker and I were the only 75th personnel still at Lingling. The others had already been evacuated. Advancing Jap ground troops were getting too close to the base.

A flight of four 75th Fighter Squadron P-40s flew overhead, heading for an alternative base at Kweilin. One of the ships peeled off and came in for a landing. He overshot, landed long, and crashed into a rice paddy at the end of the runway. The pilot knocked himself out on his gunsight, and got a compound fracture of his left arm.

You never could tell about plane crashes, especially how long it would be before they exploded. You can't tell *when* a crashed plane will explode, but you do know that most of them will go up.

I was scared crapless, and I guessed Moose was too. We wanted to get the unconscious pilot out of his plane and get all three of us as far away as possible before that happened.

Moose and I ran for the plane.

Before we got there, it burst into flames. We recognized the pilot. It was Miller and he was either unconscious or dead. He hadn't moved and the plane was already burning furiously.

We got to it, climbed up on the wings and unfastened Miller's harness, flinching back from the flames, and dragged him out of the cockpit. We got out of there in a big hurry.

They gave each of us a Soldiers Medal. But it was sad. We pulled Miller out of that fire before we got out of Lingling but the guy was killed later while he was off on another combat mission.

Our 75th took a lot of pilot losses.

"Earthquake McGoon"

By Wallace Little, Fort Walton, Florida

Airplanes were a very big part of James McGovern's life from boyhood until he was killed in Indo-China in 1954 while piloting a C-119 "Flying Boxcar" in support of the beleaguered French military forces holding on at Dien Bien Phu.

The boy, later nicknamed "Earthquake," was born in 1922 in Elizabeth, New Jersey. After school he entered Casey Jones School of Aeronautics, in nearby Newark, and in 1942, he enlisted in the US Army Air Corps, winning his wings and a commission as a second lieutenant with little trouble. After completing fighter training, he was sent overseas and ultimately was assigned to the new 14th Air Force commanded by Major General Claire L. Chennault. The 14th AF was the follow-on organization to Chennault's highly successful American Volunteer Group (AVG), commonly called the "Flying Tigers."

McGovern flew combat in P-51s with the 118th Tactical Reconnaissance Squadron of the 23rd Fighter Group formed in 1942 directly out of the disbanded AVG. He shot down four Jap planes confirmed, with another four probables.

His combat buddies began calling him "Earthquake," then added "McGoon" instead of using his real last name.

Tales about Earthquake McGoon began flourishing after he and several other former 14th Air Force pilots joined Chennault's post-war airline, Civil Air Transport (CAT). While flying out of Shanghai, China, he began building the reputation of a bar-hopper.

When fun time activities moved out of the Air Forces housing facility of Broadway Mansions (nicknamed "Bangway Mansions" by the flyers who stayed there) McGovern followed the activity closely, wherever it went. If there was no action, he created some.

Although he was no stranger to the brawls that seemed to swirl around CAT aircrews, he was not mean-tempered, and when the scrap was over, it was over. Others, as well as McGoon, claimed all they were doing was letting off steam from the stress of flying into combat areas where the Chinese Nationalists and Communists were battling it out.

On one such flight, his C-46 ran out of fuel, and he put it down on a river sandbar - and was promptly captured by the Communists. By this time, he weighed in around 300 pounds, with a girth that would have made it physically impossible for him to fit into the P-51 cockpit where he had flown his combat. The Communists kept him a prisoner for several months, then without explanation, released him, much reduced in weight. He always claimed the Reds let him go because they couldn't afford to feed him. Freed, he rapidly regained his lost weight.

When the French Government pleaded with the U. S. Government for some C-119s, along with qualified pilots, McGoon was one of a number of CAT pilots to volunteer. Their pay was outstanding for that time, but McGoon had another reason to volunteer.

"You either fight the Reds now or later, here or some other place," he said.

In French Indo-China, McGoon flew the increasingly dangerous resupply flights supporting the French military forces at Dien Bien Phu, and its surrounding outposts. Even though the Viet Minh lacked fighters, they had capable gunners handling excellent antiaircraft weapons. More than once, McGoon's plane sustained serious hits. On May 6th, late in the day, he was hit twice, losing an engine and having his control cables shot out. Seconds later, he crashed into the surrounding hills. He and his entire crew were killed.

He was cool to the end, evidenced by the calmness of his radio call just an instant before crashing, displaying the same courage he had earlier in combat.

Still only 22, he showed he had an abundance of courage - and an extrovert's desire to have fun in whatever situation he found himself. Toward the end of the war, but before the signing of the peace in Shanghai on 2 December 1945, he flew out of Liuchow to Hanoi, some 500 miles away, on a "local clearance" with several other pilots from the 118th. There, they landed at one of the Jap-held airfields. With engines running and six .50 caliber machine guns from each of the six planes aimed at the headquarters building of the Japanese military authorities, "talked" them out of a supply of French Ginger Beer.

The entire 23rd Fighter Group was moved to Liuchow in the summer of 1945. We had been scattered at a number of different bases. Each organization was bivouacked in its own area but ate at the same mess hall (large tent).

One day, my CO called another pilot, Don King, and myself into his tent. He told us we represented the 75th Fighter Squadron and would escort General Stratemeyer and his personal B-17 to Kiangwan Airdrome, in Shanghai, for the Jap surrender. The ceremony was scheduled for 2 September. We would be under the command of Lieutenant Colonel Bruce Downs from our Group. There would be pilots from each of our sister squadrons, the 74th, 76th and 118th. We would depart on 1 September and fly to a designated point to rendezvous with Stratemeyer near a very large lake named Poyang Ho, at a point where a river flowed into it. I wondered what would happen if the Japs sent up an armada to attack us. I need not have worried. If the Japanese had the fuel, they didn't have the pilots.

The flight from the rendezvous to our landing at Kiangwan was uneventful and boring. We had the throttle way back, and still did large, sweeping "S" turns to keep from running off and leaving Stratemeyer's B-17.

Strangely enough, the flight to Shanghai was uneventful until we landed and taxiied into the parking area at Kiangwan. There, we saw several P-51s, with familiar yellow and black lightning streaks running the length of their fuselages. Those yellow lightning streaks told us that some pilots of the 118th had beaten us there. But who?

I wouldn't learn until years later who had flown these planes.

A story found later in the book solved that mystery. It is in the form of direct quotes from the war-time diary of Wayne G.

"Whitey" Johnson, one of those pilots who - along with our fabled Earthquake McGoon - got to Shanghai ahead of us and the general himself.

A Pilot's Last Letter

By Jack Beaty

Editor's note: This was sent to me by Armit W. Lewis, of Colorado Springs, Colorado. He was a very close personal friend of Jack Beaty. According to Lewis, "Lieutenant John A. Beaty was a young fighter pilot from Memphis, Tennessee, who was killed on his first mission against the Japs. He was flying out of Hengyang at the time. As was customary with some, he had written a last letter that he hoped never would have to be mailed. Pilots wrote these personally, leaving them under the pillows of their beds, to be mailed if they were killed, to try and soften the blow from the much more impersonal letter from military authorities announcing their death. Here is his letter. It is dated 11 December 1943."

"Dear Mom, Dad, Sis and Bud:

"Tomorrow morning I go on what I hope will be the first of many missions against the Japs.

"I'm a bit excited, anticipating a thrill, content with my lot.

"If this first mission, and those to follow, are fortunate for me, you'll never get this. I'm confident it will never be mailed, but should the occasion arise, I want you to have a message from me a little more personal than the Adjutant General's 'REGRET TO INFORM YOU.'

"Naturally, I can't give you the details, nor do I consider them important, but I want to reassure you of my 'feelings' about the matter.

"Should you get this, consider me just as alive as when I left the kitchen to milk the cow, or as when I carried a watermelon out to the stone table in the back yard, or when I left you at the Grand Central Station that last time.

"After all, I have been away for a long time and this will be just another tour of duty, which will last a little longer, but which will end with our being together again.

"I'd hate to think of your grieving over this prolonged separation, so look at it as I do. I've always yearned for far-off places and so-called adventures, and this is exactly what I want to satisfy this yearning.

"There's a war going on and I'm where every man should be. What more could I ask? I don't have any particular aim after the war except a vague 'I'd like to stay in the Army' or 'guess I'll go to South America.'

"The main reason I want to come back is just to see you all. So remember when you miss me, that while I'd just as soon live out my normal span and see more of you all, I did to the end what I've tried to do and 'fought the good fight.'

"More than likely they'll send you some of my personal effects - my camera, my diary, my photos of you all and possibly, my personal pistol, my watch (if they find it) and so on. I've left enough trinkets behind that each of you should have a souvenir.

"Don't weep over these manifestations of my physical existence. If you want me, just sit down in Dad's chair, in front of the fireplace, about midnight, and as the little blue flames dance above the coals, I'LL BE THERE, 'cause that's my favorite place in the world, especially since I hit China and the cold weather.

"It really tickles my sporting sense that a handful of us here are holding Tojo and his midget minions at bay. If I go down, I hope my buddies get about six of them for me.

"I hope Bud doesn't get into this business.

"He will make a name for himself in a peaceful world and I'd rather he did not have his sensibilities dulled. But if he does get in, I know he'll make us all proud of him.

"It would be nice to have a closer view of Sis, as she makes her place in the world. When I last saw her, she was becoming a woman and the sight of her was good to see.

"Mom and Dad, I think the two of you are the best I've ever seen. You have given me the things I don't think I could have found anywhere else. I love and respect you more than anything else in the world and no mere separation of my soul from my body can dim that love.

"There are many people I love and whom I'd like to enjoy life with. It would take a page to name them, but you know who the most important ones are and you'll tell them good-bye for me.

"If I am (killed) I hope it will be many years before we meet again. Where I am is but a moment and these years will be sweet for you. I love you all more than I can ever put into words, so until we meet again,

"God be with you."

Jack

Chinese Bandits

By Byron Winborn, Irving, Texas

I was in intelligence in China during World War II.

I was sent to look over a Jap plane that had been downed well inside the territory controlled by the enemy. I had waited three days in Shanmen for the Jap Army to get off a coastal highway so I could cross it and walk out onto the peninsula where the Jap plane had gone down. The Jap Army had pulled its long-garrisoned troops out of their Foochow cantonment and were retreating north.

The coastal highway was not good enough to handle a Jeep, but it could handle a horse or someone on foot. It would handle me because I was walking.

My host, the Magistrate of Pingyang District, had evacuated Shanmen when the Japs occupied his town. He was my buddy.

The area was quite remote. Most of the locals had never seen an Occidental before. The elders would stand beside the trail and bow respectfully when I walked past. When doing so, scrupulously they always covered their "aggressive" right hand with the "passive" left hand. The people here had never seen automobiles, Jeeps or trucks, but everyone had repeatedly seen airplanes flying overhead. They had been thrust rudely into the mid-20th Century without benefit of any transitional period.

Finally the magistrate's scouts reported that the last of the Japs had straggled northward. It was safe to move out. The magistrate assigned a Chinese Army captain and six soldiers to us - to me and my loyal young interpreter, Willie Ho - as our personal guard. I never met finer troops. The captain and his men were armed with concealed pistols. Willie carried a carbine and I packed a .45 automatic pistol. We were not about to wear uniforms. The magistrate fitted me out with a conical coolie hat and weathered rice straw blouse.

We walked down to the highway in a few hours. We were to learn how disreputably the Jap troops had behaved, plundering and raping. They had long ago run out of ammunition. To keep up appearances they had filled their wooden ammo boxes with stones and conscripted Chinese civilians to carry the boxes. Able bodied types had long since vanished from the area. Consequently, women, shop clerks, and the elderly got conscripted for this labor. When a conscript could no longer carry his load, the Japs would dispose of him.

When we reached the highway that the Japs had so recently vacated, the first thing we found was the body of an elderly Chinese gentleman with a wispy white beard. The top of his skull had been bashed in with a rifle butt. The whole area had a weird aura. My good Christian boy, Willie, said, "Even the demons have left this place."

After walking for many *li*, we approached a village. The villagers at first thought we were the Japs coming back, so they bugged out. The captain sent two of his soldiers to overtake them and tell them that we were Americans, friends, and to come on back. Incidentally, we also wanted dinner and a place to spend the night. The magistrate was very somber for so young a man because so many of his people had been killed and raped during the last few days. The only time his face lit up was when someone mentioned that while the Japs were there, their general learned that both of his wives and all his children had been killed in a B-29 raid on Tokyo. That brought a smile to the young magistrate's face.

The peninsula we were walking onto the next day was outlaw country. For many years, my friend the District Magistrate, had wisely refrained from sending his soldiers into that area. As we sloshed on through the mud from the steady rain, Willie told me about the town that we were approaching. It was located near a mountain which was composed mostly of aluminum. The town was named Franchan, which means "Alum Mountain." Once it had been a prosperous mining town. But for the past several years the mining business had not been good, and by this time, everyone still in the area had become an outlaw of one breed or another - a robber, a bandit, or a pirate.

After several more hours of walking we crested a hill and looked out over a large valley with a mob of troops in white uniforms milling around a temple. My friend shoved me out of sight into a rest shelter. I was very conspicuous by being 5 feet and 10 inches tall, outlandishly tall by their standards. The Chinese Army captain then sent two of his soldiers out to reconnoiter. They came back and reported that the troops were what Willie called "Big Knife Bandits." Earlier, I had read books which referred to them as "Broad Sword Bandits." By either name, I was about to meet them.

I quickly learned about them first-hand. They were very clannish and wore their own uniforms topped by a hat with a red dash on it. They also had their own flag. It was a red affair with a complicated device in silver stars. They were not communists; they just liked the color red. They had their own religion and, at intervals, respectfully faced the sun and bowed with their palms pressed together in front of their chests. They robbed only the rich and the magistrates, and did not kill. They were quite well regarded by the common people. Until very recently they had been puppets of the Japs. But the Chinese Nationalist Government had scored a great coup and won their allegiance. This involved a grant of amnesty for their past sins and a cash payment in gold, one probably amounting to a few cents each. Besides, the bandits could see the handwriting on the wall: the Japs were not going to win this war.

So, since the bandits were now our allies, it was proper for us to fraternize with them. We formed our force of nine officers and men into a column and marched off down the mountain. When the bandits saw us coming, they formed a column of fours and marched out of the other end of the valley with flags flying - all 600 of them.

We entered the town. It was as crooked and cramped a place as I had ever visited. The narrow streets were hemmed in by heavily walled buildings with small, barred windows. We called on the magistrate who invited us to be his guests for the midday meal, a thought we had in mind in seeking him out at this time. After we had spent some time, about 45 minutes, with this magistrate a courier rushed in breathlessly with a written message. It said a party of nine Japs, one with a rifle and eight with pistols, were approaching the town. We allayed his fears by explaining that we were the supposed nine Japs, and the rifle was the carbine that I had Willie carrying.

After our meal, the magistrate casually mentioned that the Jap plane I was after was out on the coast. So, I thought, the pirates had been after its guns. The guns were brought to the magistrate's town and hidden from the bandits there. I told him this was good, and asked them to show them to me so I could make some rubbings of the markings on their receivers and collect one sequence of ammunition. The magistrate refused. I reminded him that I had a paper from General Chennault authorizing me to make such inspections. He still refused.

When I asked why not, he explained that the Big Knife Bandits wanted the guns, and if my party of nine men were escorted out to where the guns were hidden, the bandits would see us and capture the guns after we had moved on. I reminded him that my party had just chased the bandits out of his valley.

It was raining like mad. We negotiated for two hours before he was finally willing to make a deal. I was able to convince him that one coolie with a single small boy walking in the rain would not attract the bandits' attention. He got a boy to guide me out to the guns. I walked along behind the boy, stooped over, still wearing my coolie clothes.

The 20 mm cannon were hidden in the temple around which the bandits were milling when I first saw them.

We departed that afternoon. The trail led us up into the mountains, and it had many curves. As was usually the case, each individual walked at his own preferred rate. We would often pass completely out of sight of each other. It was a bit startling to round a curve and find myself face-to-face with a Big Knife bandit armed with an iron-tipped spear. The bandit and I would each stare straight ahead, as if the other wasn't there, pass, walk exactly four steps, then irresistibly wheel around to see if the other guy was going to start something.

The arms the bandits had were interesting and varied. Some carried antique Japanese rifles; others only the traditional big knives. Not all our allies in World War II had state-of-the-art weapons.

That evening we reached the home of the magistrate in whose bailiwick the Jap plane was down. He very courteously gave me the bed in his office and moved into his wife's quarters for the first time in 20 years. In his office, he had a large desk covered with a thick glass plate. Under the glass he had photographs of dozens of dead Jap pilots, including the one from the plane I was seeking. Mostly, the bodies were propped against a tree. It was very obvious from the fact they took no prisoners, the people in this area did not really like the Jap pilots. I was told that the life expectancy of a Jap pilot, after his plane stopped moving, was about 5 minutes. It was immaterial how good a crash landing he might have made.

The magistrate had a photograph taken of himself with his son, the captain of my guard, Willie and myself. He served some excellent beer, recently recovered from a Jap ship that the American planes had sunk just off the nearby coast.

The next morning we walked the 12 *li* over to the downed plane. The pilot had gotten lost in a storm and run out of gas. He tried to glide into a large valley for a belly landing in the rice paddies, but couldn't quite stretch it enough, and came to rest on the brim of the hill overlooking the valley.

The plane was a brand-new Tony, only slightly damaged when it bellied in. It was one of most beautifully crafted planes I had ever examined. Early in the war, the Germans had sent a complete set of drawings and specs of their ME-109 to Tokyo by submarine. They had been particularly proud of the fuel injection pump for the inverted V-12 engine. The Japs had faithfully copied the aircraft design, but threw out the design for the fuel pump, and engineered one of their own which was definitely superior. I dismounted the pump, which had at least 14 tubes sticking out of it. It was quite heavy, so I lashed it to a bamboo pole, and had a couple of coolies lug it out when we left the plane.

I got all the pertinent intelligence information in two days. The weather was getting hot. I did not relish the idea of a long walk up the coast to a river I knew about. So, the next day I asked the magistrate to charter a sea-going junk which I could ride, sailing up the coast in style. He refused. When I told him I would gladly pay for it, he still said no. I asked him why, and he explained that there were pirates in the bay. When I told him I didn't give a damn about the pirates - I had a crack, nine-man armed party to handle such things as that - he told me the pirates had a 75 mm cannon on their junk, the ammunition for it and the skill to fire it accurately enough to make my proposed trip decidedly hazardous.

I told him I'd start out walking, the first thing in the morning.

Willie and I, with time to spare, indulged in some target practice. This could be a good idea in places where the security situation was somewhat iffy. We were both good shots. The magistrate and others who watched were duly impressed.

Earlier, the magistrate had apprehended a couple of low-down robbers and wanted them taken to Pingyang to get their heads chopped off. He realized we were, obviously, the most potent military force in his sector, and since we were going to Pingyang anyway, he wanted us to take them with us. He turned the two robbers over to my captain of the guard, and got a receipt for them.

The robbers were young, very evil looking. For Chinese, they were rather tall. Both had some kind of a disease. They had been caught killing people, and as a result were sentenced to death.

The next morning we started walking north. The two robbers were treated as well as possible, considering the circumstances, but they were in rotten physical condition, and suffered excruciatingly, trying to keep up with our 10 *li* per hour pace. But if they were to travel with us, it was up to them to walk as fast as we did.

A magistrate of a village through which we passed prepared a noon meal for us, and it turned out to be excellent. A Jap ship had been sunk in the shallow waters nearby, and the Chinese had retrieved many bottles of Formosan fruit juice. It was delicious! While we were inside, the robbers' left wrists were tied only by a very light line to a doorknob out on the porch. I took it on myself to tell Willie that while I had nothing to do with the robbers, it did appear to me that they might be able to escape while we were inside. He said it would not happen. I suggested that it would be possible for the robbers either to untie the knots or break the lines easily. He said they wouldn't do it. I asked him why not.

"It just isn't done, that's why."

I don't know about that sort of thing. Had it been me, if I was under a death sentence, as soon as the door closed, I would have been long gone. But, as Willie had told me, it just "wasn't done." I guess Chinese "customs" are indeed different.

That afternoon, we moved into territory taken over completely by the Big Knife Bandits. They would swarm around us during our rest stops. I could tell that my captain was having a field day, regaling them with some kind of a story. I found out later that he would point to Willie's carbine and say that it was a super-powerful machine gun. It could fire 600 rounds "Brt-t-t-t!" just like that. The bandit leader was mightily impressed. Then the captain would say, "See that weapon the American carries at his waist?"

"A-a-h-h!"

"One volley can kill a hundred men!"

Loud sucked in breaths.

"See that armament lashed to the bamboo pole?" The bandits would crowd in close.

"Stand back! It is a poison cannon!" They would trip all over themselves backing out of the way.

As the sun set, we came off the last mountain onto the edge of a vast plain. It was criss-crossed by a network of narrow canals. There were no roads. We knew that Pingyang was only a few hours walk on the other side of the plain. I also knew that my beloved home town of Nanping was, with luck, only 7 days hard travel beyond Pingyang.

The Big Knife Bandits had captured a village at the edge of the plain. Now, they swarmed all over that place. They apparently had encountered some slight opposition in the capture, and had been obliged to burn a few houses. A Chinese Protestant church building in the village had been closed because, after all, the Big Knife Bandits had their own religion. They could hardly be expected to tolerate the competition of some off-beat sect in their own territory.

The bandit chieftain had set himself up as the magistrate in the village. He was young, well educated, and reasonably well versed in Chinese etiquette. He was making a good thing out of the bandit business, too. As was proper, he invited us to dinner. After dinner, it was always the custom for the host to rise and say, "I must apologize for the poor quality of the food tonight," even though it might have been a tasty, sumptuous banquet. Then the guest, in this case, me, would rise and make some flowery comment on how delectable the food had been. This host had not yet whipped his territory into good running order, and the food was indeed, just plain awful. So when he arose and presented the customary apology, I responded.

"It's by far the finest food I've eaten since the last time I ate."

I left it up to Willie to translate it into good Chinese etiquette.

By this time, the Chinese Army captain and I had become really good friends. We agreed we did not want to spend the night in this town. So instead, we chartered a few small canal sampans and spent the night getting poled across the plain. We could walk on to Pingyang the next morning. We certainly did not want to take those two mangy looking robbers into the small sampans with us. So my captain turned them over to the bandit chieftain, and got a receipt.

It was just starting to get dark. Even though I had nothing to do with the robbers, I had an educated guess on their current life expectancy after we left them. I figured it was about 20 minutes, if they were lucky. I did not hear any gunfire after we started out, so I concluded the bandits had saved ammunition, and proceeded in the traditional Chinese manner of their executions.

They chopped off their heads.

Death of a Hump Crew

By Dan L. Richards, Chicago, Illinois

Perhaps I shouldn't be alive today. A lot of Hump crewmen could say the same thing. Death flew alongside us a lot.

Let me tell you about one flight I normally would have been on, but wasn't. I don't recall why. Perhaps I wasn't feeling well, and the doc gave me the night off, or maybe I had just returned from an exhausting flight with another crew. We sometimes swapped crews to fill in for others as the need arose. Anyway, for some reason, near the end of my tour, I was replaced as flight engineer on my regular crew for that particular flight.

We were flying C-46s out of Chabua, a base located at the extreme eastern end of the Indian Assam Valley. It was jammed hard up against the first ridge of the Hump. Just over that ridge was Burma, and of course, whatever Jap fighters that might be in the area when our flights appeared. When this did happen, we were sitting ducks for the Japs. ATC lost a lot of planes on the Hump; some from Jap fighters, some from weather, some from lousy maintenance, some from poor navigation, and who knows what-all.

People said that the wrecks from downed planes formed an "aluminum trail" from Assam, India, to Kunming, China.

It was just about the truth except that the fast-growing jungle soon covered our aluminum trail.

Anyway, the flight I usually would have been on departed Chabua just before nightfall without me. It was a regular Chabua-to-Kunming fuel haul, carrying 55-gallon drums of aviation gas. The drums were securely tied down. Nobody wanted a "loose cannon" (read that "a loose drum") rolling around in the cargo compartment. At altitude, 100 octane gas expands and is very volatile stuff. All the crews did as mine did: we checked the drums, opening the bungs to be sure there was expansion space, then retightened them very carefully. Avgas was about as bad a cargo as we carried. All the crews, including mine, disliked carrying it. A leak could spell disaster in a hurry. But since this was virtually the only way of getting fuel to the our China combat outfits, we all did the job without too much griping.

I didn't know that my plane had taken off with a substitute flight engineer until I hit the chow hall for supper that evening. An earlier schedule had not even listed my plane or crew. Several of the guys seemed surprised to see me. They knew my ship was gone. I asked around to find out who was flying as the flight engineer, so I could check with him when they returned, to see if anything needed fixing. No one seemed to know who had replaced me. I didn't worry about that. I figured I'd check operations later and find out, or wait until the plane returned. I could meet the plane as it taxied in and shut down, then talk with the pilot myself.

All other things being equal, I knew from experience that I could expect my plane back around dawn, perhaps a bit later, depending on how long the turnaround at Kunming required. So, instead of going to a movie that night, or reading, after eating, I showered, wrote a letter home, and was in bed and asleep by 2100. I had set my windup alarm clock for 0300. I wanted to be awake and on the flight line before my plane landed.

When the alarm went off, I got up, threw some water on my face, dressed, and headed for the mess hall for a quick plate of eggs and toast and a cup of hot coffee. I finished these well before my plane could possibly make it back. After eating, I hitched a ride to the flight line, then sat around in the dark outside the operations building, waiting.

Dawn came. My plane did not.

It was nearly evening before I was able to patch the story together from several sources. It made me sick.

When I had first awakened that morning, I noticed a heavy, but thin ground fog. This was pretty common here at this time of the year. I hoped that it didn't give my pilot too much trouble getting in. Usually, a predawn breeze blew it away before the Kunming-return flights started to land. But if the breeze didn't get rid of it, I knew the hot, early morning sun would burn it off in a few minutes, and figured that if he had to, the pilot would have enough fuel to be able to hold until this happened. So I didn't worry.

I should have.

When my plane arrived at Kunming, the weather had the field socked in. The pilot held for a time, hoping for a break. He wanted to get rid of the load of avgas he was carrying because he knew how much it was needed. But the weather never did clear enough to get in, so the pilot turned and headed back for Chabua. Mission aborts at the Kunming terminus were pretty common because of the bad weather that plagued the Kunming area this time of the year. You don't like to abort, knowing the 14th is always hurting for your cargo, but you also have to face the realities of the situation there. I don't know why the plane didn't go in to Yunnanyi and unload there unless it was socked in, too.

Bucking some winds, the return flight took about four hours. Since it was still night, the crew was probably relaxed. The Japs wouldn't be intercepting them after dark. About 150 miles out of Kunming, they broke out of the weather. The remainder of the flight was under a full moon so it was probably quite pleasant. When the plane crossed the first ridge, not too far out from Chabua, the pilot began letting down from 15,000 feet and contacted the Chabua tower by radio.

Later, the tower operator told me that because of the short distance from the first ridge into the upper end of the Assam Valley where Chabua was located, the pilot descended rapidly. When the pilot called in for landing instructions, Chabua tower cleared him in, told him his was the only plane in the area. He cautioned the pilot about the ground fog. The pilot acknowledged the information, saying he didn't anticipate much trouble from the fog. He said he could see that it was thin, and already breaking up in the predawn breeze. I guess he figured that once he got down close, he could see down through it, since he said he could already see the tower sticking up through it. He would just line up with the tower off his left wing, and possibly be on instruments for the last few feet of his approach and round out, using his directional gyro to keep himself going straight after he touched down. It wasn't exactly a fun exercise, but he had done it before with no problems. Although the pilot was young - he had just celebrated his 21st birthday a couple of weeks before - he was good. I always felt comfortable flying with him. He had given me several examples of his skill and judgment.

I guess the pilot's response may have caused the tower operators to relax a bit too much too. Because it was SOP to do so, they alerted the crash crew in case it was needed.

It was!

Mohanbari was a sister base. It was sited about five miles from Chabua, a bit to the north of us. Its runway was oriented to the same heading as ours, to take advantage of the prevailing winds off the first ridge. This was to assist in takeoffs and landings of heavily loaded ships. I hadn't flown out of Mohanbari, but of course, I knew it was there, and had seen it from the air many times. Our crews were all briefed to use it if the Chabua runway was tied up in an emergency. As close as it was, we had easy access to it.

This night the ground fog had covered both bases. Although, as my pilot had commented, the fog wasn't very thick, it was thick enough to cover the cantonment area, preventing the crew from recognizing the two bases by their different building patterns. For flight crews, the essential difference was that when taking off and landing toward the first ridge, Mohanbari's tower and building area were to the right of the runway, while at Chabua, the reverse was true.

For whatever the reason, my pilot was talking to the Chabua tower, but making his approach to the Mohanbari runway, mistaking one for the other. When he thought he was lined up with the runway on final, he called the Chabua tower that his gear and flaps were down and checked. After that I guessed his attention was entirely directed at the last portion of his approach and landing.

The tower operators were also pretty relaxed. It took them a few, fatal extra seconds to realize they didn't see any navigation lights of a plane on final there. This being true, the pilot had to be making his approach mistakenly at the wrong field, with potentially disastrous consequences. When the tower tried desperately to notify the pilot, he was probably was already dipping into the remaining fog, and concentrating on the task of keeping his ship going straight. He may have realized that someone was talking on the radio but did not fully understand the words. If his copilot or radio operator understood, they were unable to get the pilot's attention in time.

The pilot passed over the edge of the field at Mohanbari and, being lined up at a considerable distance off the side of the runway, clipped a tree with his right wing. That slewed the big plane around to the right. Instantly realizing now, what his situation was, the pilot slammed the throttles forward and those two big P&W R2800s came to life and picked up immediately. He started a desperate attempt to climb.

I think he would have made it if he had a bit more room before passing beyond the *basha* area and into the trees again. It was too late. He had lost a large section of his wing when he hit the first tree. The consequent loss of lift combined with the heavy load of avgas, and the fact he had not yet built up sufficient speed to pull the nose up enough to avoid the trees condemned the crew.

Just beyond the *basha* area, his stub of a right wing caught another tree, and flipped the C-46 on its back. An instant later, still on its back, it crashed. It disintegrated into a million pieces. Of course, the drums of avgas all ruptured. For a few seconds, there was a huge ball of fire. But this died down quickly.

The crew all died instantly. I suppose that if a guy's got to go, this is a better way than most in a war.

It was still dark. The ground fog in the cantonment area was still pretty dense, even if it was thin. The crash crew chief decided no one could possibly have lived through it, so he made no effort to do anything until it got light. When the crash crew did go out after dawn, and when the fog had been blown off, they found parts of bodies strewn over a wide area. Because of this, and the intensity of the fire, the crash crew never did find everything. One of their guys found a severed head hanging on a branch of a tree, but it was so badly battered that it could not be identified.

I hated it that my crew was dead, and felt kind of guilty that the replacement flight engineer had died and I was still alive instead of him. I went to one of the guys I knew had some hooch, bought a fifth, went to my *basha* and got smashed.

I passed out on the floor. Some of the other guys who lived there put me to bed when they came in.

The next day, I had the granddaddy of all hangover headaches. But it was gone the following day. In a week, I had lost my feeling of guilt, and was just glad to be alive. In a month, I had nearly forgotten about the crash.

War is like that. While we were there, we still had a job to do. I was quickly assigned to a replacement crew, and got back into the swing of things. In a short time, I completed my tour. I returned to the States less than two months after the crash.

Medal of Honor

By John Peters, Los Angeles, California

Major Horace Carswell was the only man in the 14th Air Force to be given the nation's highest award for valor in combat, the Medal of Honor.

I was assigned to one of the fighter pursuit organizations in China in World War II. We won some honors but many in the 14th Air Force did not get nearly the recognition they deserved.

Chennault himself had been recommended by the men of his command for the Medal of Honor. Unknown to him, every member of his command signed a petition to General Stilwell but the CBI Theater commander rejected it as he rejected so many others coming from that group. Some blamed the rejections on jealousy and personal animosity between Stilwell and Chennault.

Carswell was assigned to the 374th Bomb Squadron (Heavy) in the spring of 1944, about a year after this B-24 unit became operational in China. With his experience and grade, earned in an entensely-packed three years in various positions in B-24 training units before coming to China, he was shortly appointed as Operations Officer of the 374th.

He began getting combat experience immediately. Those who flew with him testified to his steadiness and good judgment and his ability to get the maximum performance out of the B-24.

A few months after joining his outfit in China, he took off from Liuchow alone on one of a series of single-ship sweeps to hit Jap shipping in the South China Sea.

Over time, these operations began having a serious impeding effect on the ability of the Japs to bring supplies to their war effort in the home islands.

The Jap plan was to send ships through the China coastal waters to dodge Nimitz's powerful naval fleets. Chennault's counter-plan was to deny the Japanese a safe sanctuary in those waters. Sweeps such as Carswell's were part of this successful operation.

Beyond Hong Kong, Carswell found a group of Jap naval vessels. In spite of intense flak, he scored a direct hit on a cruiser and a destroyer, destroying the former and putting the second out of action.

In a later effort, he located a Jap convoy composed of a number of cargo ships escorted by destroyers. Typical of Jap cargo ships, they were heavily armed. But Carswell caught the Japs by surprise. On his first pass, he damaged one of the destroyers. On his second pass, he got direct hits on another Jap ship.

With surprise now gone, the B-24 suffered serious hits. Carswell's copilot was wounded.

Using all his skill, Carswell nursed the crippled ship back toward the China coast.

Two engines were knocked out and a third was not performing as well as it should have been.

His bombardier found his chute unusable because it had been damaged by Jap antiaircraft fire.

When the third engine failed completely, Carswell ordered the crew to jump.

Carswell remained with the plane, with his wounded copilot and the bombardier whose chute was ruined.

Carswell attempted to make a crash landing on the China coast. He was not able to get the staggering B-24 over the mountains. It went in. The plane exploded and he was killed.

Major Carswell was recognized for the skill and courage he displayed, and was awarded the Medal of Honor, the nation's highest award for valor in combat.

He was also given the Distinguished Service Cross for his earlier mission when his B-24 had destroyed and damaged the Jap naval vessels. Both awards were posthumous.

In later years, the Air Force named the base near Fort Worth, Texas in his honor.

After that, his remains were reinterred there, bringing further recognition.

Thrill of a Lifetime

By Wayne G. "Whitey" Johnson

Editor's Note: This is an extract from the wartime diary of Wayne G. "Whitey" Johnson, past president of the 14th Air Force Association, and fighter pilot in China during World War II. At various times, he flew with the 118th Tactical Reconnaissance Squadron, and the 75th Fighter Squadron, both units of the 23rd Fighter Group. Whitey is now working on a book of his own, based on his diary, and has let us use these incidents from it:

I saw General Chennault today, and talked with him. Or, rather, I merely listened to him, and answered his questions.

It was the thrill of a lifetime. I had just been sent out to the airfield, and he came along. A colonel with him called everyone out in formation. The general walked up the line and stopped in front of me.

I know he must have heard me shaking. All I could think of was that he had found out about the Jeep incident in Karachi, India, and was going to have me shot.

It was a cold day but the sweat was running down my back.

"What's your name, son?" he asked.

I told him.

"Where are you from?"

I stammered out that I was from Minnesota, and was raised up on a farm.

"Farm boys make damn good pilots," he said. "I was one, you know, from a farm in Louisiana."

I could only nod.

He asked about my training and where I was being sent.

"I don't know, sir. I don't have any orders."

"What kind of planes have you flown?"

"P-40s, sir, and P-51s."

"Colonel," he said turning away from me, "why don't you get him out to McComas? He needs good fighter pilots right now."

He turned back to me, and said, "Colonel McComas is one of my best commanders. You pay attention to what he says. We got a job to do, but I want all my boys to get back safe, and McComas knows how to do this."

The General talked with a few more men, then got in a plane and left. He had a funny little dog that trotted after him.

In a C-47 today, I flew out to a base called Suichwan, pronounced "soo-ish wan." Took a long time, and was pretty uncomfortable, but was glad to get out of Kunming, and out to a forward base where I can fly combat. I still don't have any orders, but apparently that is the way the Old Man operates. He takes care of what is needed first, and lets the paperwork follow when he is able to get time for it. His combat record shows this is really what matters, even if it does drive the "chairborne commandos" crazy.

Here I am at a forward base, and according to official orders, I am not even scheduled to be in China.

We got a young ground-pounding first lieutenant as an operations officer. He's a fussy little fat guy, and what he's doing as an operations officer I can't figure out, since he isn't a pilot. He may be just a glorified records keeper. I didn't think a fighter squadron commander would let him set up a combat schedule, and I was right in that.

He's not a bad guy or anything, just dumb about flying matters. Since he is just a first lieutenant, I don't plan to take any crap from him.

He gave me a hard way at first. "I don't know what to do with you. We can't let you fly until we get some orders on you. How in hell did you get out here without orders, anyway? Don't you know there's a war going on?"

I thought his question was stupid, but I stayed calm and answered, "General Chennault himself ordered me out here and said I didn't need any written orders. I was to report directly to Colonel McComas."

I don't know if he believed me, but he didn't object any more.

5 January 1945

Bad deal today. The 118th got the crap kicked out of it. Our squadron really took it in the rear. The guys say this is one of the worst one-day losses the squadron ever had.

Our new CO, Major Houck, was shot down. He crashed in the Hong Kong harbor. Nobody saw him get out, so he's probably KIA. Theabald also went down in the harbor, near the shore. Everybody thinks he's a goner too. Mitchel bailed out somewhere north of Canton, after we left the target area, so there is hope for him. Frank Palmer, a real nice guy, also got hit and bailed out, but this was in territory that is supposed to be safe. Sure hope he makes it. He was there with a guy who runs a radio station in the interior, and gets reports on downed guys through the system, and sends out help. He's supposed to be a newspaper man and speaks perfect Chinese. Hope he isn't anything like that gook I met in Kunming. We heard about him. These radio guys, though, are real pros, and save a lot of guys.

I'm pretty sad about our Hong Kong mission. But this will pass, everyone says.

I guess there's another big mission in the wind. I just got told to ferry a plane to Kanchow in the morning. Wish they'd schedule me for that mission.

17 January 1945.

Whoopee - so damned excited I can hardly write. Big mission from Kanchow to Shanghai! Got to fly with Charles Older, great Tiger ace. I think he's the top ace in China. I wasn't scheduled for the mission. I had ferried in a '51 yesterday, but another guy was on the schedule for the Shanghai mission instead of me. But one guy got sick at the last minute, so I was ordered to jump in his plane. Engine was already running.

What a break! This was the first raid ever on Shanghai by our fighters. We caught the bastards by surprise. There were eight planes from our squadron, but three had to turn back because of engine trouble, so only five made it to the target. Older got three in the air. They just seemed to pop up in front of him and bang - down they'd go! He's got to be the best.

We were so pushed that it was hard to keep track of what was going on and hard to stay in formation. There were Jap planes all lined up in neat rows. The Jap mechanics just stood there looking up and didn't even start to run until the planes around them started blowing up. We made four passes before they started shooting back at us.

What a turkey shoot! We were down to 100 feet or lower on each pass. Now I know why we got all that low-level training in Mississippi. At the last the smoke was so bad we could hardly see and we were flying through debris from the exploding Jap planes.

Colonel Older got the only Jap planes in the air except for Major Herbst from the 74th who also got one of them. Herbst is another ace. Heard he was grounded - don't know why he came on this mission. All the rest of the Japs planes were destroyed on the ground.

We really wrecked those Jap airfields. We could see the fires and black smoke for 50 miles after we left the target. The 74th had twelve P-51s with us over the target, but heard that a lot of the other ones from that squadron had to turn back for engine trouble. Could be from bad gas. We get a lot of bad gas, and even when we chamois it, we still get water in our tanks, and that gives us a lot of engine trouble.

The Japs know we aren't amateurs anymore. We didn't lose a plane - a few holes but no problems.

Only bad luck I got was on the way back when I got the GIs and crapped in my pants. By the time I got cleaned up after landing, I missed the debriefing. Most everybody had diarrhea, but I just couldn't hold it.

The guys said we got 80 Jap planes, confirmed. Colonel Hester said I'd get credit for two confirmed on the ground. Hester is with Wing. Heard one guy in the 74th got 11 on the ground, and I believe it. It was like shooting sitting ducks. Roy Trendeau and "Balls Out" Colins from our squadron were also on the mission. Colonel Older is from Wing also. What a great day! Everybody really excited.

We got extra-mission whiskey rations so really horsing it up.

Nobody said anything about me crapping in my pants. Maybe they don't know about it. I'm sure my sergeant crew chief wouldn't say anything.

The Diddled Dozen

By James Taylor, Grand Junction, Tennessee

Our warning network told us there were Jap planes in the area. Operations decided to send up 15 fighters to look for them.

It was a cold, crisp morning. The sky was bright, bright blue. Perfect for hunting.

My plane had been on a night mission and still had the drop tanks on it when I got down to the flight line. That was going to make it questionable as to whether it could be prepared for flight in time to make the mission. I wanted to go on this one, and was depressed that I might not make it

"They won't let me go, with those drop tanks still hanging on the ship." I told my crew chief.

"If you pump the gas out of them, they'll let you go."

"Just show me the bolt that holds it on and gimmie a wrench!"

Lopez led the 15 of us on a sweep to Lingling. Jap planes weren't anywhere around so we split up and went in different directions. Lopez took seven planes south to Kweilin. Kelly took the rest north.

When we got in sight of the field at Hengyang, they were waiting. Some were on the ground, some were taking off and coming up to fight, and a lot of others were already in the air and coming at us.

Kelly got on the radio and called Lopez: "We found 'em. They're at Hengyang. Come on up here!"

My flight peeled off and dove on the field, firing. I went down with Gadberry, Griswold and Kelly. The rest stayed up and gave us top cover.

There were so many targets. You blasted one and when it flashed out of your sights, you looked around and picked up another. You strafed anything on the ground that came into your sights.

Mostly, I fired short bursts. More than three or four seconds heated up the gun barrels and burned out the lands. Then you had no control over where the bullets went.

Ground positions were shooting at me from bunkers up and down the field. I turned on them. There was a whole lot of radio yak going on, people yelling, a lot of it unintelligible.

As I came down on a shallow strafing pass, around 50 feet above the runway, *my engine quit on me*. It just *died*, like I ran out of gas all at once. No coughing, no warning of any kind. Just silence.

I was still doing about 450 from the momentum of my dive, but with that large, wind-milling prop acting for all the world like a giant air brake, that wouldn't last long. I pulled up into a chandelle and switched gasoline tanks. No reaction from my engine. My eyes flashed across the instrument panel in an instant. All my engine gages were redlined. It wasn't a temporary fuel loss. Whatever it was, it was far worse than that. My engine was not going to restart.

I was dead in the air.

I knew I had to leave my plane, so I pulled the canopy release. It didn't release all the way. Now the jam I was in got worse.

I rolled out of the top of my chandelle at 1200 feet, much lower than I'd have gotten except for my air-brake prop. My instant plan was to set up a glide and stay with the ship as long as possible so I could get away from the scene, then bail out. But now I was in double jeopardy. My prop slowed me down which made me a sitting duck for the ground ack-ack gunners.

Explosive cannon shells hit right on my cowling. I felt three whacks on my plane: BOOM, BOOM, BOOM. There were the three accompanying puffs of black smoke. Quickly, I dumped my nose and gave up 300 feet of altitude to try and pick up a little speed and get out of the gunners' range.

Now I was down to about 850 feet and I knew I had only a few seconds left to get out of the plane safely. The canopy was still hung, so I gave it a good lick with my elbow, and it fell free over the side.

Someone once told me that if you roll your trim tab all the way forward and hold the stick back against it to maintain level flight, then when you were ready to get out, all you needed to do was turn loose of the stick and the trim tab would suddenly dip the plane down and that would pop you right out of the cockpit. I tried that but, at my slow speed, there was no "pop." Now I was really scrambling to get out of that plane any way I could.

I went out, still in a sitting position, and only about 400 feet above the ground. The tail of the plane eased right by me, going about the same speed I was. I could have reached out and touched it. I pulled the D ring on my parachute and sat there, looking at the ring in my right hand. Then I felt a big jolt. I looked up and saw nothing but white over my head.

"It worked!" I said, aloud, with much relief.

It was my first jump. They never gave us any practice at it. I looked down and saw that my plane had pancaked onto the ground and had started to burn, sending up a dark, oily column of smoke.

I said, aloud, "I'm coming down right in that fire."

It was kinda close. I landed right alongside of it. My parachute canopy drifted into the fire and burned. The Japs were so close I didn't have time to get my special escape kit out of the back of the chute harness. I just yanked the entire harness off, threw it into the fire, and my helmet after it, then started running.

They always had told me, "If you go down, head for the hills." That's where I started going. But I didn't get far. I saw a dozen Jap soldiers coming over the top of the next ridge, rifles ready, and bayonets fixed. They were spread out, making a sweep of the field where I was. I noticed a little shack off to my left. There were no tall weeds or bushes or anything to hide in or behind.

I hit the dirt.

Flat.

The soldiers kept coming. The closer they got, the flatter I got. I was like a snake stretched out in the shallow grass. They looked right over me, and started shooting at the little shack, pouring bullets into it. They thought I was inside, hiding. When they were now no more than ten feet from me, and still coming, I knew they were going to step on me.

I jumped up in their face. It scared them nearly as much as it scared me.

I held my hands up. When they got their wits about them they surrounded me and started shouting commands at me in Japanese. They took my gun, my watch, my Air Corps ring, and a small cameo ring my sister had given me for Christmas, a part of a pack of cigarettes, and a box of Red Top matches.

The matches were what really fascinated them. The Japs had little thin matches, like flat toothpicks. To strike them, they had to hold three of them together so they wouldn't break. Then they had to find a place on their match box that had enough phosphorus left so they could get a fire. My matches were all square and they lit the first time you struck them. The Japs really loved those Red Tops.

I heard a roar overhead and looked up. Lopez and his eight ships had arrived, and they joined the air battle.

After the war, I learned what happened to the rest of the flight. Weldon B. Riley got lost. He bailed out about 80 miles north of Chihkiang, but managed to get to that base safely. Andrew Jackson Gadberry was wounded and bailed out near Hengyang. He later got back to the squadron okay. Robert P. Miller was killed. Nobody knew what had happened to me. Eventually I was put on the list of men Missing in Action.

The official record of the mission said:

"Taylor stayed with Kelly until near the end when Kelly warned Taylor of Japs above and he pulled out but he missed Taylor who was not seen again."

About two months later, my folks received a letter from my old buddy from cadet days, Hugh D. Wilson.

This is what Hugh wrote:

Dear Mr. and Mrs. Taylor:

I've just received word of Buddy's death which was a big shock to me. I know he was a great loss to you, too, for he was fond of his family. He spoke of you so often and intimately that he made me feel that I knew you well.

I have missed him a great deal in the past 10 months that we have been separated. I have been trying to join his squadron for a good while but was never able to do so.

I hope it will give you some comfort to know that he was killed in actual combat rather than on a training mission as so many of our boys are lost. I understand he had a grand record up until that time, of which I know you are proud.

I was so pleased to get your Christmas card.

Please, know that I am sharing your sorrow a great deal.

Sincerely, Hugh.

But of course, I wasn't dead. I was in a small group of captured Air Force men separated from all other prisoners and taken back to Japanese homeland.

We called ourselves the Diddled Dozen.

Maj. Don L. Quigley	75th FS	Marion, Ohio
Capt. Donald J. Burch	7th FS CACW	Address lost
Lt. Walter A. Ferris	16th FS	Troutdale, Ore.
Lt. Lauren A. Howard	8th FS CACW	Franconia, N. H.

Lt. Harold J. Klota	8th FS CACW	Deceased
Lt. Freeland Matthews	8th FS CACW	Florida
Lt. Vernon Schaefer	770th BS CACW	Kimball, Minn.
Lt. James E. Wall	530th FS	Charlotte, N. C.
Lt. Sam E. Chambliss	529th FS	Silver Springs, Md.
Lt. Samuel McMillan	26th FS	Bloomfield, Ct.
Lt. James Taylor	75th FS	Grand Junction, Tn.
Lt. James E. Thomas	26th FS	Deceased
Sgt. James P. Meeham	792nd BS	Address lost
Sgt. Don Watts	Cargo	Indian Harbor Bea, Fl.
Sgt. Fred Carlton	25th BS.	Ft. Jones, Ca.
Sgt. Carl Rieger	25th BS	Jonesburg, Mo.

Quigley, CO of the 75th, and Watts, who was accidentally dragged out of his plane while dropping cargo to the Chinese Army, had been held in Hankow under guard but not in jail. Oddly enough, both came from Marion, Ohio.

Meeham, Burch, Thomas and I also had been held in solitary confinement in Hankow in a kind of half-basement of a building used as a prison. We were filthy, lousy, unshaven, and unwashed since we had been captured. On 28 December 1944 we were taken to the Yangtze River boat dock where we were met by Quigley and Watts, neat and clean and well groomed, and put aboard a river boat bound for Nanking. At Nanking we boarded a train for Shanghai where we rode a truck on to a POW camp near Kiangwan Air Base.

The camp held about 1,200 men, including Marines and civilians captured on Wake Island and some of the North China Embassy guard. There was also an Italian crew of a boat scuttled in the Yangtze River being held there.

In our group were Air Corps men captured in China between July 1944 and April 1945.

On 31 December 1944 the six of us were placed in an end room of an empty barracks at the POW camp. Carlton, Lankford and Rieger from a B-29 crew joined us. They had come in the day before from Hankow where they had been held. The Japs forbade us to talk to anyone else in the camp but we could unload on each other all we wanted to.

After being cooped up in solitary confinement, I had lots to say.

Matthews, Shaefer and Ferris joined us on 18 February 1945. That made 12 of us - the Diddled Dozen - and on 15 April, Howard and McMillan came in. The entire camp began a move on 9 May that would take two months to complete, with our final destination being Japan itself.

After five days of riding boxcars we arrived near Peking where they put us in two warehouses. We slept on the concrete floors.

Chambliss joined us 23 May, with Wall and Klota on 6 June.

The Japs loaded us back onto boxcars on 19 June and we headed up the tracks into Korea. We got to Pusan and, after five days there, we were crowded into the hold of a waiting ship.

We made a very dangerous crossing of the Strait of Korea which took a day and a half, and landed at the southern tip of Honshu Island on 30 June.

The next day we boarded another train and headed over to the Pacific coast. At Aomori, the five enlisted men of our group were taken away, as were the civilians and the Navy doctor, William Foley. We protested strongly but it did no good. The five spent the rest of their time in Japan working in a surface iron mine.

The rest of us were put on a ferry at Aomori for Hokkaido where we boarded another train and went north for several hours to some little place where we spent the remainder of the night. At noon, the next day, they called out all prisoners who were pilots. They put us on another train and we headed back south again to Sapporo where we were taken to a large frame building and kept under guard for the remainer of the war.

We had hoped to be in a prisoner of war camp but they kept us separated from the other military and confined us to one large room in a frame building on a small Japanese Army base at Sapporo.

There the Diddled Dozen remained until we were returned to United States military control on 11 September 1945.

"China Dew" Brewery

By Robert T. Smith, Mesa, Arizona

It didn't take long to get real tired of the local Chinese drinks.

Their rice wine was terrible. Plum brandy was even worse. They didn't have beer. Once in a very great while we got a ration of beer from the States at the post exchange.

One afternoon, pondering the drinking problem, a buddy suggested that the alcohol the doctor had in his dispensary would make a good drink if we mixed it with lemonade powder they was used to make the drink we got at the mess hall. Of course, there was no way we could talk the doctor out of his alcohol.

So, one of the others came up with the idea of distilling the alcohol we used in the place of gasoline in our vehicles. We stewed around with the idea for a while, trying to figure out what all we needed to do the job. One of our squadron members, Sergeant Steckle, told us we would need a large copper vat, a steady and even source of heat, plus a water source to cool the coils and condense the alcohol.

That old Yankee ingenuity came into play!

Steckle and some others made a vat out of copper. They installed a fill port and copper tubing outlet. They got a P-51 coolant gauge to monitor the cooking temperature.

Next we had to have a steady, even fire. A B-25 deicer tank was used to hold about 20 gallons of 100 octane aircraft fuel. This was piped to a burning jet, similar to a gas stove. The burning jet was installed in a 55-gallon drum, which we in turn pressurized with a tire pump. Then we installed a brass on-off valve in the line just above the jet, placing it in a .50-caliber ammunition box.

How to cool the mess? We discovered a small spring on the hillside above the building where we located our still. Its gently flowing water was cool. Lacking any pipe, we decided to use the old Chinese method of bamboo piping. We cut out sections of bamboo poles and fitted them together.

We made a small reservoir on the hillside and ran the bamboo pipe from the reservoir to the cooling tank, a distance of 150 feet. The installation was now complete.

The only thing left was to give it a try.

We did. The results were interesting.

We fired up the stove and watched while the temperature started to rise. Just a short time later, we had the distinct pleasure of watching distilled alcohol drip from the cooling coil. In a few minutes, we had about a quart.

The squadron doctor said we would have to let him check it out to see if it was safe to drink. A couple of days later, he told us that it was okay. We tried it, cautiously at first. It tasted like "white lightning." It was much too strong, alone.

So, we concocted a recipe of synthetic lemon powder, sugar and water. This made a syrup that we could cut with more water, to make a suitable mix for the alcohol. Using a Stateside whiskey bottle, we put in approximately onc cup of syrup, one cup of alcohol, and filled the bottle the rest of the way up with water, and shook it well.

Lo and behold, we had a "fine" drink. It tasted a lot like a Tom Collins.

We named it "China Dew."

Then we proceeded to supply all our squadron members with our new beverage.

Before long, other units heard about it, and wanted some of our "China Dew" and asked how to make it.

We had a good thing going for a while. Later, while we were stationed at Kweilin, we brewed many gallons of the stuff.

One day, disaster struck.

As we were working up a batch, the whole damn thing blew up. It burned three of us. We ended up in the hospital with some first, second and third degree burns.

That ended the famous "China Dew" brewery.

But the memory lingers on.

Incidentally, I am not the Robert T. Smith who was a member of the Flying Tigers and has written several books on his exploits.

I build radio controlled model aircraft, and I always wanted to build a scale model of Flying Tiger Smith's P-40, number 77. In my research before building it, I learned that Smith lives in Van Nuys, California. I plan to contact him soon.

"Flying" Crew Chief

By James L. Shannon, Houston, Texas

As a staff sergeant crew chief, I soloed in a C-47 one day, with no authorized pilot on board. It had to be my most daring experience, in China - or anywhere else for that matter.

It was in September 1942, at a base named Cho Lum Pol, actually, Chui-Lung P's airfield, near the city of Chungking.

A new radio operator, Corporal Charley Sherman, had just come in. My plane was a C-47 that was named "Fujiama Foo Foo." Sherman was helping me change spark plugs on the engines when we got an air raid warning. A 1-ball went up, and I started moving. You never saw cowlings go on a C-47 so fast. I got the engines turning over, running smoothly before the 2-ball, the second level of alert for an impending air raid - and I'm looking over my shoulder for our pilots.

I did have a bit of experience flying the C-47. For several months, my regular pilot, Major Wayne K. Richardson, lacking a co-pilot, had been using me instead. The major let me get quite a bit of right-seat time. During this duty, I handled the controls a lot. So I knew how to handle the plane in the air. I even flew with Major Richardson to Chengtu when Jap bombers hit our airfield. We usually worked with the radio station at Peishiyi. We'd fly up to Chengtu, and stay until it was safe to return to our base. Then we'd fly back home.

But when Lieutenants Art Welling and Jack Champion arrived, I went back to my regular crew chief duties.

By the time the 3-ball signal was raised, I was plenty worried. I just knew the Japs were going to hit the base. Unless we got this C-47 off the ground, it stood a good chance of being destroyed - maybe Sherman and me with it. I also knew it was a 15-mile ride from head-quarters to the flight line, and that meant it would be a long time before the aircrew arrived.

I was getting desperate. Finally, when no pilots showed up, and with me itching to fly the C-47 from the left seat anyway, I taxied out and took off, and headed for Chengtu. Poor Charley hardly knew what to do, other than just sit there. He looked very much out of place in that right seat. I had to perform most of the copilot chores too. Charlie did handle the radio for us.

After we got into the air, Charlie contacted Shorty on the radio network the AVG had left in place, and sent a message on what we were doing, to be relayed to our air office at Chungking.

As I said, I did have some experience with the C-47, but not in the left seat.

On takeoff, I learned quickly that unless I came in quickly on the rudders, and did it without over-controlling, Fujiama Foo Foo would swing wildly from one side to the other as we gathered speed for lift off. However, even if it was a bit ragged, we got off okay.

While we were in the air, a pair of Chinese-marked P-43s went by on each side of us. If they had any concern, they never showed it. They went on about their own business.

In time, Shorty called us back and gave us an "all clear" back to Chiu-Lung P's airfield. So we headed back.

As I was letting down near the field to enter traffic, I spotted a staff car. I figured I was in deep trouble, especially since I couldn't see any bomb damage around the airfield. I was afraid that whoever was in that staff car would accuse me of taking the plane up and endangering it and our lives, when there was no real cause for concern.

Being upset didn't help my flying much. I missed my first approach, and had to go around. The second time, I found the slot, and surprise of surprises, I greased the plane in for a fine landing, something the regular pilots might not have really appreciated, as bounce landings were not all that uncommon in the C-47, even with experienced pilots at the controls.

My two lieutenants, Welling and Champion, were waiting to meet me, but they didn't show me much enthusiasm. Old Charley was shaking. I was sweating as we rode into town, wondering what was going to happen to me.

Surprisingly, I was never court-martialed. I kept my stripes. Afterwards, I almost wished the Japs had bombed the field, and done some damage. I'd have felt better about taking up the C-47.

Anyway, it's an experience I'll remember always, even if I forget everything else that's happened to me since.

Editor's note: After the war, Jim got on with Delta Air Lines, and flew with them for 30 years, getting plenty of left-seat time. But it is doubtful that any of his experiences with Delta compare with his first C-47 solo while in China.

My Ship Quit On Me

By Armit W. Lewis,
Colorado Springs, Colorado

Editor's note: This is verbatim from a diary kept by Captain Armit W. Lewis, covering the period 27 October 1944 through 7 December 1944. He describes his walking out after parachuting from his disabled P-40, well behind Japanese lines in China.

27 October 1944

Ship quit on me over the railroad south of Hankow. Made it to the bend below and bailed out there. Landed about 400 yards from my ship, in tall weeds and about two feet of water. Lay low until dark, hearing Jap planes fly over. After sunset, took a homing on a barking dog and waded through weeds to a village where Japs missed me by about two minutes. Left with guerrillas on boat and traveled SW most of the night, walking and boating. Got into a village in center of lake and put up there around daylight. General Li Hsien Lin is a good name to remember.

28 October 1944

Slept most of the day, getting up to eat about six times. Had a note from Li Lin Tien, who speaks English. Saw transport and Lilly go over about 1700. At dark went boating again to another village, one we had visited last night, and talked to Li Lin Tien, who said it would take about a month to get out. Slept three in a bed at Mr. Wang's house. Heard Smiley was killed and buried near Maien Yang.

29 October 1944, Sunday

Up at 0700, another transport over. Talked with Li again. Saw six P-40s high around 1130. Pulled out around 1500 with four boat loads of soldiers for escort. One Jap PT, flying low, went over us to the SW at 1315. Boat is propelled by a woman, at least 70 years old. Have a nice Jap overcoat Li gave me. At night, had another brush with a Jap patrol on the river. Walked about eight miles, then changed boats. Rode all night, am now in the hands of the 4th Army. Ron Tsin Tsang is still with me.

30 October 1944, Monday

Out in lake this A. M., pulled up to a village to eat. If I don't die from overeating, I'll be ok. From all indications, it will be a month before I get back to Laohokow. The crowds of gaping and staring people everywhere we stop are the most unpleasant things that I have. Had my customary boiled eggs for breakfast. Moved on, in the P. M., by boat to a place west of the lake and north of Paluchi. Met by another band of guerrillas who took me over a couple of places. Took pan bath, which I needed!

31 October 1944, Tuesday

Stayed around here most of the day. Ate a fine meal at some farmer's house. Now if I don't get the GI's I'll be ok. Ron Tsin Tsang left me this afternoon. Left on a horse about 1500, then boat, then horse, then boat. Traveled until around midnight when we put up at some lone farm house. Mosquitoes bad. Raining a little bit.

1 November 1944, Wednesday

Left by boat early this morning. Much rain and fog. Took horse in the boat also. Most of the afternoon and late into the night, rode on boat to the north end of the lake above my name. Slept in village on straw covered mattress. Finally found myself on map. Guess I'm following the same route Greg and Beneda used five months ago.

2 November 1944

Foggy this morning. In the village, up to a breakfast of rice cakes, noodles and bread. Guess we ride a while now. This rain has made the walkways very muddy and slick. My butt gets sore from riding, but it's better than walking. Rode most of the morning in fine sunshine, coming into another village around noon. This one held by the Communists. Will put up here today, and get out tomorrow, I hope. Took another bath, and had my extra clothes washed. Cooked my own eggs and cabbage. They had a radio station here and a boy who speaks a little English.

3 November 1944, Friday

Cold and cloudy this A. M. Was hoping to get going, but it seems there are Japanese patrols to the north, so it looks as though it will be tomorrow morning before I get out. Greg spent five days here, Beneda three. Cooked my own breakfast again, of cabbage, eggs and rice. In the afternoon, shaved with what appeared to be a butcher knife. Walked around the village with Shar Kuei. Fixed eggs, rice and sugar in the evening. Hear that there are two other Americans at Li Hsien Lin's. They will be welcome.

4 November 1944, Saturday

Rainy and cold this morning, but still hope to get going and on my way. This staying in one place is getting me nowhere. Finally left with a 30-soldier convoy, Mr. Goo Gam Pien, and about eight women. Mr. Goo and I were on horses. A miserable day, cold, muddy and rainy. Pulled into some place at noon to eat - quite a large town, named Sinco. Went on, but now had an umbrella. Traveled late into the P. M., finally arriving at some place where we put up for the night. My boy has become quite adept at cooking my eggs, rice and sugar.

5 November 1944, Sunday

Rainy and cold again this morning. The Chinese captain and I had a fire built to keep warm. Pulled out in the afternoon in cold rain - sure is miserable traveling. Rode for about four hours, then at dark pulled into another barn-like building to sleep. Had the usual eggs and rice and had a GI (bowel movement), the first in three days now. Guess it will be about eight more days until we get to Li Hsien Lin's.

6 November 1944, Monday

Up this morning to find a blue sky overhead. But it soon closed in, so I don't hold much hope of today's weather being an improvement over yesterday's. Left around 1000 hours, then stopped about a mile away and waited until 3 P. M. Then I started a ride I will never forget. We rode until 0300 the next morning, horses slipping and sliding around, with it raining and pitch black to boot. Crossed the big river at midnight, then rode some more, and finally, put up at some farm village.

Boy, was that sack ever welcome!

7 November 1944, Tuesday

Up and away about 0800, pulled into a place that's supposed to be two *li* from Headquarters. Ate noon chow here. Every time I ask Mr. Goo where we are I get about 10 different answers. Not raining today, but we do have a high overcast. It is not too cold now. In the P. M., a man came over from headquarters, and I went back there with him. Found their place is quite nice. Also found out it is about 10 days to Li Hsien Lin's and another 10 to Laohokow. Talked with Mr. Wang, who speaks English. Most of us turned in rather late. Had a haircut. ID'd a Jap airfield under construction at Q35 R36. Transport center. Changkang

8 November 1944, Wednesday

Slept warm and well last night. Had my usual fan tan and eggs for breakfast this morning. Guess I will get out of here tomorrow. The people, rather, the officers, gave me a welcome party in the forenoon. Everyone made speeches, and I was presented with a fine Jap flag and Samurai sword by Lo Tsun. Ate lunch at the regimental commander's, a fine meal. Slept some in the afternoon, then went to a drama at night, made another speech and saw a Chinese opera. To say the least, it was a bit hard to understand! After I had gone to bed, some farmers from the next village came visiting, bringing me eggs and chickens.

9 November 1944, Thursday

Another bright day, a fine day! Cooked my breakfast of meat and eggs, rice and sugar. Hope to get back on my way today. Ate a nice meal at noon with Liu Fun, Lo Tsun, Hwang Hai Pin and others. Some more villagers came with gifts of chickens and eggs. Just before we left in the afternoon a large crowd gathered. I made another speech and was presented with a flag. We finally got under way to the popping of firecrackers. It was a fine day for walking, so I walked all the way. We traveled until after dark, making about 20 *li*, then pulled up to a village, cooked our supper of eggs, pancakes, and greens. Mr. Hwang and our guide, Mr. Tsun, ate with me. Slept fine at night, with the exception of having to get up two or three times to stop the chickens from crowing.

10 November 1944, Friday

A nice day again. Mr. Hwang and I ate chicken for breakfast, and are getting ready to be on our way. I walked for quite a way. Then we met another company of the 4th Army soldiers coming back from a brush with the Japs. We stopped with them for a while, then went on. Walked 20 *li* this morning, then pulled up a couple of hours to eat. Rode horses in the afternoon until about dark, then pulled up to sleep in the nicest farm house I have seen. Washed my feet, ate, and turned in.

Had a four-poster bed, but covered with straw. The mountains are now to the north and west of us. Slept nice and warm at night.

11 November 1944, Saturday

Another nice day. Guess we will get up to, and cross the Jap-held road today. Saw a B-29 fly over this morning. Walked about 15 *li*, pulled up to eat and rest, then walked about 15 more *li*. At dusk, got on the horse and we crossed the road without incident. Covered about 50 *li* today. Pulled up about 2130, ate the usual soup, Mr. Hwang's pancakes and arrowroot. Walked quite some distance today. In spite of a bitter cold wind, the traveling was rather pleasant. We have been fortunate lately in having such nice weather.

12 November 1944, Sunday

Up early this morning, left the village where we slept as it is too near the Japs. Traveled about two miles, then pulled up to another village to eat breakfast. Saw one Jap plane flying over from west to east early this morning. Then later, saw another, a Lilly, going the same way. Rode the horse the rest of the day, getting near the lake in the evening. Really tired and hungry this evening. Ate another one of our chickens, egg cakes and such. Went to bed early. This is some sort of a headquarters. Met a Chinese brigadier and his wife. Village is very muddy and dirty. Rats running around overhead all night. A baby squalled most of the night, which made sleeping difficult.

13 November 1944, Monday

Slept rather late this morning. Weather very cloudy and sprinkling rain, so I am afraid traveling will be bad. We stayed in this place all day, which is ok. The rain got worse and kept up all day. Had two meals today, one in the evening rather nice, with wine, sweet cakes, and such. Mr. Hwang and I talked much of the day. His favorite subject was politics and mine was airplanes. Talked into the night, then finally turned in, once more to the sound of nocturnal rat fights overhead. Guess we'll get to Headquarters, or Li San, about the 20th.

14 November 1944, Tuesday

This morning, up, took a much-needed bath, and changed my clothes. It has stopped raining, but now we have a high overcast. Mr. Lo Tsun came in. Tomorrow morning, he is going to headquarters, too. The commander here gave me a new Jap pistol and some photos which I am very glad to have. Mr. Hwang and I talked to General Li Hsien Lin in the A. M. Guess it takes another six or seven days to get from here to Li San, then about nine more to Laohokow. Slept in the P. M., then to pass the time, wrote some memorized poetry. Raining tonight. The people here gave us some tinned oranges which we ate with our supper.

15 November 1944, Wednesday

Up rather early this morning. It is cold and rainy, but I guess we are going to go on and try to cross the lake today. Waited around for some farmers until about 1500, then started out without them. Crossed the lake with a company of soldiers, pulled into the village on the other side about 2100 at night. The sky was clear and the stars were out. Maybe tomorrow will be a nice day. Had a late supper with Mr. Hwang, then turned in. Rather cold at night.

16 November 1944, Thursday

Up early this morning to find the day bright and clear, which is welcome. Had the boy-acting-doctor put some medicine on a small boil on my chin. Guess we will leave this afternoon and cross the road to the north. The Japs are very near this place. Left in the afternoon and walked until sunset, then mounted the horse. Had a little trouble crossing the road - had to wait about an hour while some Jap convoys passed. Finally crossed and went on another 12 *li*, then put up for the night. Very cold at night now, but warm enough during the day. Our boys fixed supper for us after we had gone to bed, so we got up again and ate. At 1600, saw a couple of Lillys flying toward Hankow. Later, at night, heard explosions from that direction.

17 November 1944, Friday

Cold and clear this morning. Had the boil on my jaw opened and fixed. Shaved myself also, which was needed. Slept most of the morning on a straw sack in front of the house. Left about 1700, walked about 10 *li*. Crossed one river, then another, and next, crossed a motor road without incident, except the horse fell off a bridge. Walked and rode until about 0300. My boy Shao Tsun was sick, so I let him ride my horse for a while. Was very tired when we finally pulled up. E Hwa fixed me some meat and eggs, then I turned in. One of the peasants with us was sick also.

18 November 1944, Saturday

Slept until about 1000 this morning, then ate, and we started off again. My feet are sore from walking, but I let the boy ride the horse again, since he is still sick. Had the boil on my chin repaired again, and now it is just about well. Mr. Hwang feeling better than last night. He was pretty ill then. Only went a short distance today, then pulled up at a small headquarters where I saw my first Jap. He had been captured by the Chinese and was working for them. Moved on another short distance, then put up in a small village. About 1500, saw four airplanes bombing the railroad. Can see the mountains over to the east where the headquarters is. Mr. Hwang and Shao Tsun feeling bad again this evening. I ate quite a large supper, then turned in early. There is a new moon now, which will help us in our coming night travels.

19 November 1944, Sunday

Up this A. M. to find the sky overcast. I hope the weather holds good until we get to Li San in two or three days. We left around noon, crossed the ruined motor road and then pulled up to eat lunch and rest. Started east again about 1600. Another Val overhead. Rain threatening, and the weather giving the Val a hard time. We're lucky, though. The rain never came where we were. Crossed the river, then crossed the railroad just after a north-bound train. Traveled until around 0200 or 0300, then pulled up 20 *li* from Li San. Mr. Hwang fell into a small river just before we got to the village, and was completely wet, and cold. I fixed some eggs and meat, then went to bed around 0400. Came about 50 *li* today, but am not as tired as I expected I'd be. We are in the mountains now. The farmers told us that the boys missed the bridge they bombed yesterday.

20 November 1944, Monday

Up around 0800 today. Ate eggs and sugar cakes, had my boil repaired again, and am ready to be on my way. A very nice day to travel. I walked a way, then rode 30 *li* to headquarters. Here I ate an enormous American-style meal. Had eggs, steak, oats and catsup. Had a bottle of Jap beer, which was flat, but had a good flavor. Met Mr. Hwang Hi, who speaks English. I was put up in the room where Major Eggers stayed while he was here, on his walk-out. There are many mountains around here, and the scenery is very beautiful. Ate egg foo yung at night, then turned in. Had a comfortable bed. Before going to sleep, had a long talk during which my stay here was outlined for me. The people here are very nice to me, but I want to be on my way. I want to start for Laohokow by at least the 23rd.

21 November 1944, Tuesday

Up rather early this A. M. to a bright, cold day. Had a good American-style breakfast of rice, eggs, coffee and meat. Got the radio set up today and contacted BC1. Sure was glad to get them. Talked for a few minutes. Told them I would be there in about 10 days. Then went to a meeting of the farmers. This was in the P. M. I gave a speech, then went back to the house and tried to get BC1 again, but was unsuccessful. At night, I went to a very large meeting, where I again spoke. Then back to the house, had some jam rolls, got the news on the radio, and finally turned in.

22 November 1944, Wednesday

Up this A. M. to contact Dolphin on radio, but only had R-1, S-1. Talked to one of the staff members most of the morning, then in the P. M. went to a welcome dinner where I was well-filled with Jap beer. After that, went to a drama, where I sang two songs. Afterwards, had my usual jam and biscuits before turning in. Finally, to bed.

23 November 1944, Thursday

Up and packed this morning. Was given a hari-kari knife, some photos and intelligence to take with me. Talked with Mr. Tsun, the delegate from Yenan, had my picture taken with a farm group, reviewed a regiment of troops, gave them a short speech and after bidding farewell to Mr. Hwang and Cha, was on my way. Have a new translator, a Mr. Sheva, who is going with me now. Walked 10 *li*, ate lunch, and walked on in the P. M. Walked and rode all afternoon, crossing the railroad again just after dark. When we heard some shooting, we stopped and rested for a while, then moved on. Went another 20 *li*, and pulled up to a village to sleep. Had some cookies and some tangerines the farmers had given me before turning in. Went a total of 70 *li* today.

24 November 1944, Friday

Up around 0800 today. Am going to try to walk in the Chinese shoes today, as my others are about finished. Walked about 20 *li*, met General Li Hsien Lin on the way. He told me a bomber had crashed near here on the 21st or 22nd. Stopped at the 2nd Army Headquarters in the morning. We stayed here. Slept and read in the afternoon, then at night went to a dinner party given by General Wang. Was told it would be safer for me to stay here tomorrow so we could meet the Nationalist troops more easily. So I guess I will have to stay, though it isn't to my liking. Went to bed around 2100. Talked to two of the Jap prisoners in the A. M. One seemed ok, but the other was one of the most stupid-looking men I'd ever seen.

25 November 1944, Saturday

This morning, finished reading my detective story. Then I got up and had a barber give me a dry shave. I don't recommend it. The WX is fine again today, but guess we will stay here until tomorrow anyway. Slept most of the afternoon. At night, went to a meeting of the officers under General Wang. A nice meeting. I gave a speech and answered their questions, then the boys sang and danced, so I sang my usual two songs. Had an American-style cook prepare some cereal before going to bed. The American food sure is good.

26 November 1944, Sunday

Cold and rainy today, but we got on our way in spite of it. We had 10 Jap prisoners, and 100 Chinese soldiers. Very bad weather, making travel difficult. Went about 20 *li*, crossed the motor road, then went about 20 *li* more and pulled up at a Regimental Headquarters. We're now about 10 *li* from the wrecked B-29. Built a nice fire and ate a good supper, so we are pretty comfortable. Very cold at night, though. One of the Jap prisoners is having a little trouble keeping up with us. Too bad! Guess, if I'm lucky, I may get to CB1 in six days.

27 November 1944, Monday

A strong cold wind from the northeast this morning, but the clouds broke in the A. M. and the sun came out. Rode and walked about 20 *li*, then rested and as is becoming usual, ate an American-style meal. Then went on for another 20 *li*, crossed the last Jap highway without incident. A biting cold wind was blowing from the north all day, so it was better to walk than to ride. At night, arrived at a place where the Nationalist troops were supposed to meet us. Had a supper of eggs, fish and the usual two big plates of wheat cereal. Had a smoky fire in the room which we had to put out so we could sleep.

28 November 1944, Tuesday

Rainy and cold this morning. A bitter wind from the northeast. We rode about four *li* in the morning, where we met Mr. Gee, the magistrate. A major from the Nationalist Army came and ate a big breakfast with us. We discussed the situation while eating. Guess it will take us four days to reach Cheyong, where we can get a motor bus to Laohokow. The Nationalists sold a few bullets to the New Fourth Army troops. Didn't go anywhere today. I am glad, as it rained all day, in addition to being quite cold and windy. Sat around the fire in the afternoon, talking, eating peanuts, and what not. I drank one of my bottles of Jap beer. Mr. Sway and I went to bed about dark. I sure like these warm old sacks!

29 November 1944, Wednesday

The Nationalist major came by this morning and had breakfast with us. Very cold and windy this morning, but we got on our way, after saying good-bye to the New Fourth Army people, Mr. Sway, the cook, etc. Took the horse with me as always, as well as our two boys. Rode and walked in the A. M., disturbed once by shots and bullets whistling over our heads. Just the Communist soldiers saying good-bye, however. Around noon, pulled up at a village, fixed my own meat, eggs, and wheat cereal. I miss the American-style food I was having! Walked most of the P. M. until about an hour after dark, when we crossed a river and pulled up to a village to sleep. The major wanted me to sleep in the same bed with him in the room with the Jap prisoners, but no go. My boys and I slept in another room.

30 November 1944, Thursday

A little snow this A. M., but not raining as it was last night. Up to a fire and a breakfast of greasy eggs and cereal. Walked and rode most of the day, about 40 *li*. Came to a small village. Put up behind the counter in a store, after first warming myself and washing my feet. Had a nice pine fire. There is as much difference between the Nationalist Army and the New Fourth Army as between night and day. Watched some of the "corrective treatment" - punishment by hitting a soldier's hands. This army is no good at all.

1 December 1944, Friday

My two boys from the Communist Army left me this morning, taking the horse. I hated to see them go. Had a very cold wind today, and snow. Walked nearly all day. The boy who was carrying my pistol became lost, and while he was riding to catch up, he lost my gun. This Nationalist Army is the most disorganized bunch I have ever seen. Got to headquarters at Cimboo at night. We found a man here who speaks English. Slept in a room where they kept a fire going all night, so I was warm. Sent a telegraph to Laohokow telling them I would be there on 4 December, but I doubt if I make it. Cleared off at night, and now we have a bright moon.

2 December 1944, Saturday

Up and ate in the room with the fire. That heat felt good this morning. Now they tell me it will be December 5 when we get to Laohokow, so I sent another telegram. They have not found my pistol. Left ahead of the Japs and stayed ahead of them all day, stopping only a couple of times, including once in a very dirty village, where we were supposed to eat. But I raised hell, so we went on. Found out later that they wouldn't feed the Jap prisoners at Cimboo. Cold and clear today, no clouds at all in the evening. Had a charcoal fire, and my usual wheat cereal, meat and eggs. The Chinese major and I are going to sleep in the same room here. Went 60 *li* today. Have a new horse, or rather, a mule. Got to Cimboo. Eating my usual wheat and sudzas. Bought two pair of socks.

3 December 1944, Sunday

Up and walked 12 *li* to where we ate breakfast. Then on to a place on the highway where there was supposed to be a phone to Laohokow but of course it didn't work! This is some army post! Found a nice boy here who speaks English. He is from Hong Kong. Talked with him a bit, and took his address. Rode 15 *li* more in the evening. My left foot is hurting considerably. Now I'm paying the way, using New Fourth Army money! Slept in a small temple-like building at night. We left the Japs behind here. Very cold but clear. Did 60 *li* today.

4 December 1944, Monday

Up before sunrise this A. M. and walked 15 *li* to where we are now fixing breakfast. Ate in the dirty village, then rode horse most of the day, seeing two B-25s and six P-40s fly over. Sunshine and cold all day today. Rode and walked 75 *li* (or 15? Can't read my diary) to Chyang, to the headquarters, only to find no auto, as I expected. They say the road is just too bad. Was treated very nicely by the city though. Had a nice Chinese supper and slept in the hospital. Talked to Carter at Laohokow, and was sure glad to talk to an American again. Tired at night. Someone here speaks English.

5 December 1944, Tuesday

Cold and snow this A. M. We started off in a *whagar* (sedan chair), eating peanuts on the way. Made 90 *li* today, got into a small town on the river in the late evening, put up at the city government quarters. An English teacher here wanted me to give a speech to his students this evening, but I refused. I was just too tired. Had a

Chinese meal with the major, then turned in. Had a charcoal fire and a good snack.

6 December 1944, Wednesday

Up early this morning, and gave a short speech to some of the students at this town. Ate breakfast with the major, then left in a *whagar*, completing 20 *li*. After that, rode a boat down the river for 25 *li*, then another 15 *li* with a rickshaw available, but didn't use it. Got into Franchan where I caught up with Major Eggers and the other Americans. They sure looked good! We went over to Sianyang to the American missionaries to eat. Had mashed potatoes, chops, gravy, ah, lovely! Cold at night. With Eggers, slept in the American mission across the river.

7 December 1944, Thursday

Franchan-Laohokow. Up at the mission and bought $1500 (Chinese) worth of charcoal this A. M. so we could keep warm. Had breakfast, then Major Eggers and I went to see General Ho to pay our respects. Met the Jeep from Laohokow, then went back to the mission, ate and left, after saying good-bye to Eggers, Bigler, and Peterson. They are on their way back to Tao Shan. I don't envy them. Had a rough three-hour ride to Laohokow, but made it ok. There was a B-25 there. I will leave with it when the weather at BM5 breaks. The B-29 gunner came out with me also. Had a swell meal - with pie. Ate with Carter and the boys for the evening meal. Wrote a letter home, talked to Reed on the radio, read some magazines, then went to bed.

8 December 1944

Laohokow-Lingshan (at last). Still have the habit of getting up early, so I did it this morning also. Went over to see General Wang, the Chief of Staff, then when I came back, learned the WX at BM5 was ok now. One of my ex-students was there in a transport, so I got aboard and he brought me to Liangshan. The place sure looked good! Saw all the boys, found some changes had been made: Bill is now the group CO; Bennett the wing CO, and I am now the squadron commander. I have a hell of a lot of mail to read, and answer. Started to go to a show at night but decided to read my mail instead. Turned in around midnight, after shooting the breeze.

Paxton up at Ankang.

Buffalos, Evil Spirits and Missionaries

By Schumann Cherry, Sun City, California

The Chinese had the interesting belief that evil spirits followed them around, trailing just behind them, trying and do them harm. They also believed that these evil spirits couldn't make sharp turns. So they often built the walls of their homes in a zig-zag, as well as their shorter bridges.

Then came the modern world. They tried this idea out there, too. They thought that if they could run across the runway in front of a fighter or a B-25, the prop would cut up the evil spirit, and get it off their tail.

Unfortunately, they were not accustomed to the speed of these machines. Their timing wasn't all that good. More than one believer ended up getting for himself what he wanted for his evil spirit.

It was pretty messy.

The mess hall would occasionally serve us a slab of what they called steak - a piece of water buffalo. Man oh man, was that stuff ever tough! It was like old shoe leather.

Once we left the States, mostly we ate out of our mess kits. Over time, I lost my fork first, then my knife. There were no replacements. At Ankang, all I had left was my spoon. But losing the knife wasn't all that much of a loss anyway, at least on those steaks, when we got them. It would have taken a knife a lot sharper than them to cut that meat. So, I used a flat stone to sharpen the edge of my spoon. Then, holding the meat with one hand, I managed to cut it into manageable size pieces.

Next came the fun of chewing. The more you chewed, the more it seemed to grow. That's why you cut it into small pieces.

After chewing a while, you sort of gave up and just gulped, swallowed hard, and let your stomach worry about it. It wasn't very tasty, either.

I made out okay. Our food wasn't exactly top-of-the-line, but we had no alternative. We didn't get any Stateside food. All our chow was provided by the Chinese Government, through its War Area Service Command. It was about four times what the Chinese soldier was given to eat, but it wasn't much by our American standards.

The Post Exchange was another gripe we all had. Back in India, the New Delhi Commandos had very complete and full post exchanges. The shelves were loaded. The further away from Headquarters you got, and the closer to combat, the less the PX had on its shelves. In Assam Valley, just before jumping up over the Hump, you could still get quite a bit, but it sure wasn't like the rear areas.

In China, even at Kunming, all we ever got was the leavings from India. And for the real forward bases, the combat outfits, it was worse.

Sometimes, we'd get six Baby Ruth bars, half a carton of cigarettes, a package of razor blades, and a couple packs of Lifesavers. That was it. No soap, or shaving cream, and not even writing pads.

Whatever ration you got, you bought it, even if you didn't want it, like the cigarettes for the non-smokers. If you didn't want the stuff, someone else was hurting for it, and would immediately buy it from you. Besides, if you didn't buy it, the traveling PX officer from Kunming wouldn't give anybody else a crack at it. He said it all had to be taken back and returned to the Exchange. I'll bet! I got some doubts that anything he took back with him ever ended up in the Exchange.

To get to the town of Ankang from our base, you had to take a ferry. It was off limits to us but there was a bunch of helpful missionaries there. We'd arrange with them to invite us over occasionally, then after dinner and talk, we'd take off and hit the town.

There wasn't much the MPs could do, because there weren't many of them, hardly enough to control a small crowd. Besides, the base had no jail, and our CO sure wasn't about to send anyone to the clink at Kunming, because he needed all the troops he had.

Air Service Command outfits were always short-handed, and over-loaded with work. So, we kept our little excursions to Ankang under control, and the MPs ignored them. It worked out okay, because the commander didn't want to lose anybody, and we wanted to be able to get to town once in a while. It was sort of a Mexican stand-off.

Most of us really didn't want what the local talent had to offer anyway. We were all pretty well briefed on the dangers of what were called, then, "social diseases." That was enough to discourage us most of the time. Especially because if we caught some of the diseases, we were told, we would not be permitted to return to the U. S. after the war. We would have to spend the rest of our lives in China.

Bob's Letter Home

By Bob Frazier (Dec)

Note: Bob Frazier, 75th Fighter Squadron, wrote this letter to his folks while stationed "somewhere in China" during World War II. His widow, Bonnie, believes it will strike a responsive chord in the memories of others who served there, and they will enjoy reading it.

Since I left the States, I have been quite a few places, Mom. I will try to trace my route since I left San Francisco, and got to China, and tell you a few of the things that happened. Now I am not telling you these things to worry you, Mom, because I think if I was going to get killed it would have happened a long time ago, because I was in a lot more danger then than I am at the present.

First of all, I left the States on the *Maraposa;* that's a sister ship to the *President Coolidge*, which you wrote got sunk. She was in our convoy also. So was the *President Johnson*. For our protection, we had the cruiser, the *Phoenix*. At first we were supposed to go to the Philippines, but the Japs had just about conquered it by then, so we headed for Australia. We reached Brisbane on 31 January 1942.

We stayed there for a while, then came down to Melbourne. We waited there for some time to pick up some more troops, then sailed around the west coast of Australia to Fremantle and Perth. We waited there, too, until the aircraft tender *Langley*, some freighters, and some troop convoy ships joined us. When everything was ready, we left and headed for Darwin, all bunched together in a convoy. I had been moved off the *Maraposa* at Melbourne, and was on an old Australian boat named *Katooba*.

Some of the boats that were in our convoy were the *Danube, Holbrook, Sea Witch* and others whose names I have forgotten now. For our protection, we had the *Langley, Phoenix* and the English boat named the *Exeter*, a ship that helped sink the German pocketbattleship, the *Graf Spee*. We knew we were heading into trouble when we started for Darwin. Japs were bombing it every day. When we were about two days out of Darwin, a Jap observation plane spotted our convoy. From then on, things began to happen. We had about four hours to get ready because it took that long for the Jap observation plane to go back and tell their bombers and torpedo planes where we were.

Our convoy split up and each boat went in a different direction. Our tub, which was the oldest boat in the convoy, was also the slowest in the bunch. So we didn't have much of a chance if the Japs had wanted us very badly. But they were after the aircraft tender and the *Sea Witch*, and maybe another one of our combat boats, I am not sure. I guess about 200 of our sailors on the *Langley* were killed or drowned when it was hit, and it sure made me feel bad, because just a few days before, we were all having a good time together in Perth. I knew lots of those boys that went down in the *Langley*.

After the bombing was over, we couldn't get in at Darwin, so we headed for Batavia, on the Island of Java, but the Japs were closing in on it, too, so we changed directions and started for the Island of Ceylon. We finally pulled in to Trincomalee, which is a port on Ceylon. We refueled there, then went on to Colombo, which is another large port in Ceylon. We were there for some time, then finally started again, this time for Bombay, India. For some reason, we couldn't get in there, either. So, we continued on to Karachi, India, where we finally docked. When we got off the boat there, I was sure glad to see land and get my feet on something solid again, for a change!

Remember, all this happened in February and March of 1942, over a year ago. There was probably a little bit about it in the papers back home, but you have forgotten all about it by now.

For the first four or five months while I was in India, things were pretty easy for us. We had to wait until we got new equipment and that takes a long time to come from the States. Here are some of the places I've been since arriving in India: Bombay, Karachi, New Delhi, Agra, Aliahabad, Dum Dum, which was near Calcutta, Dinjan Tiensucie, and Chabua.

The last ones are all airbases in Assam, which is an Indian province up close to the Burma border. Dinjam has probably been bombed by the Japs more than any of the others. I was in Dinjam on 26 October 1942, when the Japs came over with 54 bombers. We didn't have any warning at all. They were almost overhead before anybody knew it. Then you should have seen us guys hitting the slit trenches and tea patches - any place where was a hole, somebody got into it!

They only got one American out of the whole bunch, but they did kill quite a few Indians. These people just don't seem to have enough sense to take cover. The Japs bombed us on the 26th, 27th, and the 29th of October. During that time, our antiaircraft got 17 of their planes, so it wasn't a bad trade - 17 for one.

On 11 November, we took off from Dinjam and flew over the Hump into Kunming, China. When you fly over the Hump, which is the only way to get from India to China, you fly over the Himalaya Mountains, Burma and the Burma Road. The Hump is the worst airline route in the world. Even on the southern route, there are mountain peaks 15,000 feet high. If you are ever forced down, there is no place to land. If you bail out you probably land in enemy territory, so all in all, you haven't got much chance if something goes wrong. You also run the chance of getting shot down by Jap Zeroes. The Japs have a base at Lashio now. This is within the flying range of the Hump for their fighters. Until we retake Burma, and the Burma Road is reopened, flying the Hump is the only way we can get our supplies to China. Every day, scores of transport planes fly the Hump. But even with all this, we still can't get enough stuff up here. And, when the weather is bad, we don't get anything at all, as our planes can't fly then.

When I first arrived, there were only about 300 American soldiers here. But now there are about 1,500, with more coming in every day. Even at that, we are way outnumbered by the Japs. Of course, there are lots of Chinese soldiers, but they haven't any equipment to fight with. I doubt very much if they want to fight very badly anyway.

You probably read in the papers about the Chinks and Japs fighting down on the Salween River. This is in the southern Yunnan Province. Now I am at Kunming, which is also in Yunnan, but about 200 miles from there. Every time the Japs try to get across the river, we send our planes down there, and they bomb and strafe 'em. Then the Japs withdraw. You can probably read in he papers about the Chinese Army chasing the Japs back across the river. If it wasn't for the American Air Force, the Japs could take any part of China they wanted. If we just had an Air Force that was big enough, we could chase the Japs completely out of China by ourselves.

"This airbase at Kunming used to belong to the American Volunteer Group (AVG) before we took over and most of the AVG members went back to the States. You have probably seen pictures of our pursuit planes with the sharks (mouths) painted on the front end.

The Burma Road that you have read so much about runs through Kunming and I have been on it for a short distance while I was riding in a truck. I have also flown over it. It is just as rough and crooked as it is shown in the pictures of it that you have seen.

I have also been to Chungking, which is now the capitol of China. I flew up there and was supposed to be there for one week, but our plane had engine trouble, and it was two weeks before we could get the spare part to fix our plane, and leave.

There are other places in China where we have airbases. I still have not been to them, but I will probably go on up before long. Some of these bases are at Kweilin, Changyi, Nangi, Yangling, Mengtze, and others. So if my address changes later on, you will know about where I am. I think it will be Kweilin. I believe I am to be transferred to the 75th Fighter Squadron before long. Kweilin is where that outfit is now located.

This air force in China is known as the 14th Air Force now. General Claire L. Chennault, the AVG chief, is the head of it. It is made up of the 23rd Fighter Group, which has the 74th, 75th, 76th, and 16th Fighter Squadrons in it. Whenever you read in the papers about the 23rd Fighter Group doing something, it means that the 75th, as one of its squadrons, is probably involved. I am also involved since I'll be in the 75th. Whenever you read about Canton, Hong Kong, Nanking, and Tienstsing or any of the smaller Jap-held Chinese towns being bombed, you will know that our boys in China did it.

About all the news in the papers you sent me from back home is about the Marines fighting in the Solomons. This is about 1,000 miles farther from Tokyo than we are. If we could just get the equipment, we could bomb Tokyo every day.

The majority of the troops in (censored) are a few Americans with the Chinese armies, but not many Chinese armies (censored). All our fighting is done by bombing and by combat between airplanes. We had no Americans involved in hand-to-hand combat or ground fighting.

Well Mom, I guess I had better sign off. I don't want you to worry about this letter. I just thought I would write and tell you some of the things straight so you would not get them mixed up. Maybe this will mix you up even more, though (ha ha). Please write and tell me if you get this without it being cut up too much by the censors.

There is not much use in you asking me questions about what is happening here, because the censors probably wouldn't let me answer them.

All is well.

With love - **Bob**

Shanghai Nights

By Wayne G. "Whitey" Johnson

Editor's Note: These direct quotes from the diary of Wayne Johnson explain how he and Earthquake McGoon got to Shanghai for the Japanese surrender ceremony ahead of General Stratemeyer.

"The first night in Shanghai was a sensation. We didn't know how much trouble we'd get into but we were sure exposed to the advance surrender party which had followed us in. Six P-51s from the 23rd had escorted General Stratemeyer into Kiangwan on the 1st, for the surrender ceremony the next day. When we arrived, we had parked our planes like we owned the world. They had to see them when they taxied up to the parking area. We figured we might get court-martialed for it, but it would probably be worth it.

"The ride from the airport to downtown Shanghai can't be described. Hundreds of thousands of cheering and flag-waving people! When McGoon and I landed, it was pretty scary. The Japs were still around. We heard that the Generalissimo had asked that the Jap authorities keep their troops armed until the Americans and Chinese Nationalists could take over, to avoid rioting, and not to surrender to the Chinese Communists or to guerrilla troops. When I saw all those armed troops I started to wonder if McGoon's idea of flying right on up to Shanghai was such a good one.

"We sat in the planes for a bit to see how the Japs reacted, but they just stood back. A little Chinese in a black kimono ran up and down and nearly got his head chopped off by our props. He spoke good English. We couldn't figure out whether he was the Mayor or the Mayor's assistant. He got us a truck for the ride into the city.

"The Jap troops were everywhere, marching in formation, but they never looked at us. The Jap general was really pissed off when we booted his ass out of his fancy suite in the Park Hotel, and took it over for ourselves. The Park is a beautiful hotel, with no war damage. The Jap general refused to give us his sword, though. He was not about to surrender to lieutenants. And we didn't want to press our luck.

"The hotel was lavish. We didn't know where they got all the good steaks, fish and fresh vegetables. Sure didn't look like war was hell here.

"Hope Operations can fix us up for some flight plan and orders. McGoon said we had to land because of bad weather, but hundreds of miles is a long way to divert because of bad weather.

"After we had a long bath and a rub down by some beauties, McGoon started looking for some 'poon tang.' The masseurs were strictly that and weren't interested in any loving. Didn't take McGoon long to get back with a couple of girls in tow. They said they were White Russian, and had been interned since 1937. They worked as waitresses for the Jap officers, but said the Japs never bothered them. The Japs preferred Chinese or Korean girls - something about it being below their station to settle for a white girl.

"These girls were appreciative of us liberating them. WOW!

"When Generals Wedemeyer and Stratemeyer got in and found out what we were doing, they put a stop to our charging meals and booze. We got the word that the U. S. had no contract with the Park Hotel, and didn't know who would pay the tab we'd run up. We had to vacate our suite, too, for the generals. The whole 'situation' came to a halt when we got orders to get our asses back to Liuchow immediately. Sounds like the stuff was about to hit the fan.

"Now that the war is over, though, they don't get too excited about our getting 'lost' in bad weather. McGoon was sticking to his story about how his compass was out, and since he was the flight leader, the rest of us had to follow.

"We got back to our squadron, and everyone was getting orders to transfer, or to go on ferry missions. Even the CO didn't seem much concerned about our absences. He didn't want to hear about our escapade, either. He just said, 'Don't give me any of that crap. I know what you foulups were up to!' But he did log our flying time.

"Then he said, 'For your little R&R, I'm kicking your asses out of the 118th. I've got to send someone to the 75th, and you just elected yourselves. You're being transferred. You can stay in China till hell freezes over. If you like that Chinese stuff so much, you can stay and enjoy it some more while the rest of us all head for home.'

"Don't know whether he was really mad or not, but here we are, over in the 75th, and it is only a couple of hours later. The word that we'd been to Shanghai got around in a hurry, but McGoon and I thought we'd better not do any bragging and better play it cool. We said we were on a secret mission for the surrender and couldn't talk about it. No one in the 75th seemed to care much, however . . ."

Some pilots were already talking about taking their discharges there and staying on in China. Others wanted to go home first, and after a visit with the home folks, come back and fly transports in post-war China. McGovern was one of those electing to continue his flying in China, a choice that ultimately cost him his life. I can't help but think that if he knew he was going to die, he would have preferred it happen the way it did rather than from the boredom of sitting at a desk in some corporate office.

"Earthquake McGoon" was that kind of a man.

Looking for Dad

By Bruce Doyle, Gainesville, Florida

My father had been shot down in French Indo China. That's all I knew. I picked up that much when I was a kid from a newspaper clipping my mother had. It said he was shot down on June 20, 1945 while flying a B-25. That was all I knew for more than 40 years.

Mother would never talk about my father, about his death, or about their life together after they got married. I didn't know how tall he was, whether he was left handed or right handed. I knew from his school papers that he graduated from high school in 1940. I figured he was about 25 years old when he was killed. I had only one picture of him, showing him graduating from Bombardier-Navigation School.

I didn't know when he got in service, but at least I knew it had to be around Feburary 1945 because I was born in June 1944. I had seen a photograph of him holding me. I knew it was a few days before he went off to China. As I grew older, it was in the back of my mind to find our more about him.

I read every book I could get on the air war in China. I thought my father had flown with the 341st Bomb Group in China; they had B-25s. From year to year, I wrote off to Maxwell Air Force Base or to Wright-Patterson, trying to get information but I always came up with dead ends.

Then, one year at the Air Show at Titusville, the Doolittle Raiders came. I thought, 'Ah ha. They flew their B-25s into China after they hit Tokyo. So maybe some of them knew my father.' As it turned out, they all got to China in 1942 and most had left by 1943, a year before my father arrived. So, none of them knew him.

In March of 1988, the people who ran the Titusvillle air show brought in men of the American Volunteer Group, the original Flying Tigers. So I figured, 'Well, these guys were in China real early but maybe some of them knew my father, somehow.'

I went down to the air show and met Ed Rector. I talked to Tex Hill and Wayne Rich. They gave me some names and addresses, and an old Jing Bao Journal. I wrote letters and asked the Journal to put a notice in, saying I was looking for someone who knew my father, and to please write me and tell me anything they knew.

I heard nothing.

My mother's birthday was in November and I wrote her a letter, telling her about a guy from the 60 Minutes television show I had met in school. We were studying the Vietnam War. He told me about a girl he knew who was lamenting the fact that she had never met anybody who knew her father in Vietnam. She visited the memorial Wall in Washington and met somebody there who knew him in Vietnam and she was really happy.

I said my father was killed in Vietnam but his name was not on the Wall. He had been killed over there 40 years earlier.

I wrote mother. I remember sitting in my library and writing it. It was a very tough letter:

"Mother, I know what happened to my father was very painful to you, and a great loss, but there comes a time when I've got to know. My son, your grandson, who is now 20 years old, and your granddaughter, know nothing. I know nothing. I want to be able to tell them. I want to know when you got married, how you and my father met, were you scared about him going overseas, did he have any misgivings, what were his plans for after the war if he came back, did he want to stay in the service."

My wife walked into the library. I had tears in my eyes. It was really draining, emotionally.

I sent the letter. Mother called up, like bingo. That was what burst the balloon. She wrote that she was going to sit down with a tape recorder and tell me all about it.

The next month - it was Christmas - my brother-in-law called and said my mother had fallen and broken both her hips. So I went down to see her and talk to her. She said she though my father was in the 491st Squadron and that there were two other brothers. She said all the brothers married girls named Jean, like her name.

In the third week of April, I was taking my daughter to school one morning. This was rare for me, because I worked late at night and my wife usually took her to school. So I was coming back home, driving down the street about 10 blocks from home, and a man turned turned his car in at the school bus yard. As he turned, I saw a decal in his rear window and it was a 14th Air Force Flying Tiger Association decal. I would not have recognized it if I had not gone to the air show and met some of the Flying Tigers.

I made a U-turn, crossed four lanes of traffic, and followed the car into the parking lot. I jumped out and ran up to him and said, "Were you in a B-25 outfit in China, back in World War II?" I told him about my father.

He shook his head. "No. I was an insider. We repaired airplanes. I wouldn't know about your father. Sorry." His name was John Benson.

However, he happened to have a couple of *Jing Bao Journals* with him. "Here, take these," he said. "And here's an Ex-CBI Roundup. I've got a lot more of these things at home. Meet me back here Wednesday afternoon and I'll bring them to you. Maybe they'll be helpful."

I was in the parking lot waiting for him when the he came back. He must have had a stack of about 40 *Jing Bao Journals*. It was in that stack that I found the key that unlocked the door. It was the 1986 Directory of the 14th Air Force Association. There was page after page of names and addresses of men who had been in China - but there was no way of knowing which of them might have known my father.

I took a ruler and underlined every member of the 341st Bomb Group. That was about 350 or 400 names out of the list of about 3,000 names. I waited until after five o'clock to get the cheaper long distance telephone rates and started calling.

Oscar Harper in Jacksonville, Florida was the first guy I called.

"Do you happen to remember a guy named George Doyle?" I asked. "Do you remember an incident in the 491st, a plane being shot down with two brothers on board?"

He said, "I really can't say I do. I remember the name 'Doyle,' but I came home in March of 1945 so I wasn't there at the time you're talking about." He wrote down a name on a piece of paper and handed it to me. "Here's a man who might be able to help."

I called the man, a Colonel Willabridge, living in California, and asked if he remembered someone named Doyle in the 491st.

"Sure, I remember Doyle," he said. "He was a navigator."

But the colonel described "Doyle" differently than my mother had described my father. Also, the colonel could not remember any plane named the "Three Jeans" which my father flew in.

After I hung up, I began to think about this other Doyle. I told myself that, if there was another Doyle in the 14th, maybe they ran into each other. I looked to see if the other Doyle was listed in the directory.

There was only one other Doyle listed. His named was T. W. "Buck" Doyle and he was living in Arlington, Virginia.

I'll never forget that call as long as I live.

It was Friday afternoon and I called around five o'clock. I got a recording. At the beep, I said, "My name is Bruce Doyle. My father's name was George Doyle. He was killed on or about June 20, 1945. I believe he was in the 491st Bomb Squadron, 341st Bomb Group. Would you happen to have known him, and would you please call me if you have any information you can give me."

About 45 minutes later, the phone rang and my wife, Susan, answered it. She looked up at me. "You better get over here. This guy sounds excited."

So I got on the phone. This wonderful, deep voice said, "Did I know you father? Hell, yes, I knew your father! And what is this nonsense about him being in the 491st? He was with me in the 11th Bomb Squadron. Besides that, I've been looking for you since 1953 to give you one of our Flying Tiger scholarships worth about $5,000."

I made some silly joke about not wanting to go back to school and we both laughed.

He said, "Another thing, my wife, Dolly, says she knew your mother when your mother was here in Washington and you were just a little baby."

My mother's father had been a member of the Roosevelt administration and lived in Washington. My mother, apparently, had known Dolly then.

"I'm having a Memorial Day party up here," Doyle went on. "Would you come up as my special guest?"

I told him that sounded great. He didn't give me a lot of specific information about my father but he did say they were together in the 11th Bomb Squadron. So I wrote another letter and made about

400 copies and sent each out with a picture of my father in it to guys in the 11th.

Late the next day, I got a call from Leroy Marks who said he was the crew chief on the plane my father had taken off in on the morning he was killed. He confirmed the date my father was killed and gave me other details, including the names of the two brothers on the crew.

I got a call from the copilot of the plane that took off right behind the one my father was in. He said, "As a matter of fact, that mission and the four planes that took off that morning are in our squadron history called *'The Record.'* I'll send you a mimeograph of it."

Then the letters started pouring in, and more phone calls. Someone sent me a copy of *"The Record"* with a picture showing the mission my father was on. It was a famous picture. It had appeared in *Air Force Magazine* and in China Lantern It was the only mission pictured in the book and it was the one my father was killed on.

One caller said, "Did you know your father was a fine basketball coach?"

"I had no idea," I said.

"Yea, he coached the team that won the China All Stars game."

Several others sent me pictures of the games and this was the first I had ever seen of him, since the one showing him holding me just before he went to China. I felt delighted and so proud of him.

The letters kept coming in.

The Record shows my father was assigned in September of 1944. Its narrative ended in February of 1945. From then until the end of the war, nothing.

I wanted to find out as much as I could to fill this gap from the men who were there at the end. One of the men, Ed Conji, lived in Bradenton, Florida. The last time I was coming home from visiting my mother in Naples, I stopped by his house. He was the first person I met and shook hands with who had known my father. He was on that final mission. It was a thrill talking to him. Finally, after all those years, and all the heartache and maddening frustrations, the mystery was going to be solved, that painful blank spot in my life was going to be filled in.

I had known my father had died but I didn't know how. That bothered me very much. I didn't know if he had suffered, if he got shot out of the air, or what. So now, I was shaking hands with a guy who could tell me just what happened to my father on his last mission.

Ed Conji told me that the mission had gone in on a skip bombing attack to get a bridge. They had delayed action fuses on the bombs so that the planes could get away before the bombs exploded.

Coming on the bridge, Conji said, they faced an ack-ack blockhouse defending the bridge. The plane ahead of my father's opened up with it's .50s on the blockhouse. At the same time, that crew felt their plane lift, which meant that one bomb had been released. Because of some confusion, they delayed in dropping their second bomb.

The bridge was not destroyed because the second bomb overshot it. That meant the second bomber, with my father in it, had to come down and make a bombing run.

The gunners in the blockhouse were waiting.

The crew on the first plane blamed themselves. They thought that, if they had done their job right, the gunners in the blockhouse would never have shot down my father's plane and my father might still be alive.

Theirs was a beautiful thought but I certainly didn't consider them responsible. War is like that. But to see these men make such a soul baring admission to a man they had never met before, so that he could begin to understand what happened, that showed a beautiful concern for others.

For the first time, I began to feel that I really knew who I was and where I came from. Learning about my father was like learning about myself.

I went to Arlington to Buck Doyle's Memorial Day party. He sort of adopted me as a son and I adopted him as the father I never knew. We became very close. Without realizing it, Buck began calling me by my father's name. It gave me goose bumps. I began to have the strange feeling of being in my father's presence.

Soon after that, both Buck and my mother both died.

Both had lived just long enough to help me find my father.